Th

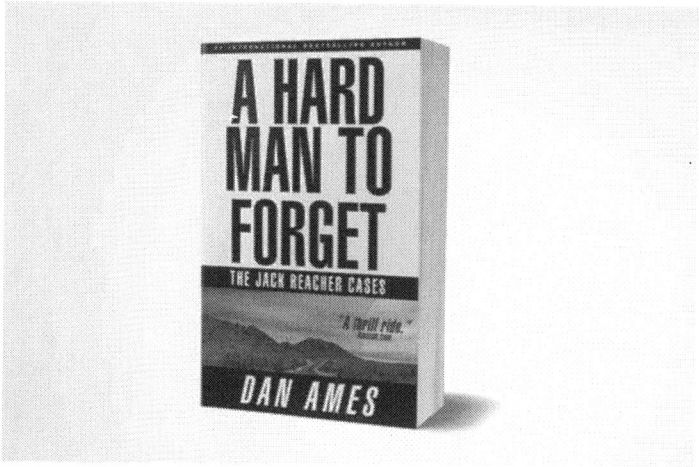

A USA TODAY BESTSELLING BOOK

"A fast-paced thrill ride."
-Amazon.com

MW01538997

THE MURDER STORE

A WALLACE MACK THRILLER #2

DAN AMES

Copyright © 2017 by Dan Ames

THE MURDER STORE is a work of fiction. Names, characters, places and incidents are either products of the author's imagination or used fictitiously. Any resemblance to actual events, locales or persons, living or dead, is entirely coincidental.

All rights reserved.

No part of this publication may be reproduced or transmitted in any form or by any means, electronic or mechanical, without permission in writing from the author or publisher.

WALLACE MACK THRILLERS

"Ames is a sensation among those who love fast-paced thrillers." -*Bookiio*

"Ames reminds me of the great thriller writers - lean, mean no-nonsense prose that gets straight to the point and keeps you turning those pages." -*Author Robert Gregory Browne*

"Not since James Patterson has someone taken the serial killer genre and turned it on its blood-splattered head. Ames writes with a smooth confidence and his characters will stick in your mind for a long time after you've finished reading. Probably well into the night." -*Amazon.com*

FOREWORD

For special offers, free ebooks, exclusive content and to hear about new releases, sign up for

The Dan Ames Book Club at

AuthorDanAmes.com

THE MURDER STORE

BY

DAN AMES

"Have you ever made a just man?"
"Oh, I have made three," answered God,
"But two of them are dead,
And the third
Listen! Listen!
And you will hear the thud of his defeat."

-Stephen Crane

OPEN FOR BUSINESS

1

Somewhere in cyberspace

The content of the website whistled through the cyber switchbacks, bounced between hundreds of free wireless hosts and encrypted IP addresses before it was distributed to a small collection of pre-paid subscribers.

The first customer to log on was a man who had inherited a highly successful and profitable plumbing supply company in New Jersey. He had been the sole beneficiary of his father's estate, which included an impressive investment portfolio. The man had nothing to do with the actual plumbing supply business or its day-to-day operations. He simply reaped his share of the profits, along with the dividends of the stock holdings.

Most of his time was devoted to a hobby.

The hobby was by no means cheap.

And although the dividends from his trust fund had typically been more than enough to cover all of his normal expenses in the past, they were nowhere near enough to cover the costs of his secret pursuits.

His private passions were very, very expensive.

Which is why he had been tapping into his inheritance account's principal and watching with a sort of sick fascination as the total amount dwindled.

But he had no intention of stopping.

It was how he spent the majority of his time now. The truth was, his workday and work week entailed no actual work. His day-to-day calendar was completely empty as the company was run by a very capable set of managers who knew the business far better than he did, and had become visibly annoyed when he first inherited the business and tried to become more involved in the operations. After a discussion with the senior managers of the company, it was decided that he would be more of a consultant, only called upon for the most dire of emergencies.

In the intervening years, there had been no emergencies.

So with a completely bare calendar, he was left all of the free time in the world to indulge his dark obsessions.

The man followed the very specific and highly complex instructions to log onto the site. The protocol, which always arrived in an encrypted email, changed every time The Store was refreshed with new inventory. The man was comforted by the complexity of the operation and took it as reassurance that the people behind the enterprise were extremely careful and knew what they were doing.

He couldn't argue with the results.

It took several minutes to complete the verification process, which included a retina scan, and then the site appeared on the man's enormous, plasma computer screen in his home office. The door had an internal deadbolt so no one could surprise him as he did his shopping.

The screen went live and the man slowly released the breath he hadn't even realized he was holding.

With crisp graphics, neat copy and high resolution photos, the product page looked like any other major retailer's website. The difference was the type of items being offered for sale.

The man's breath caught in his throat, and a sexual surge pulsed through his body as he took in the images before him.

He didn't want to rush this, but nearly everything he saw he wanted to buy.

Forcing himself to slow down and relish the shopping experience, he painstakingly reviewed all of the photos, and read each product description several times over, comparing and contrasting features, product attributes and price.

The images excited the man to the point of distraction. His breathing became rapid and shallow as he fully surrendered to the addiction that consumed him.

Eventually, he realized he had fallen completely in love with the face of a beautiful nine-year-old boy.

He let out a slow breath, closed his eyes, and made his purchase.

2

Southwestern Colorado

It had been a long winter for the coyote mother. Her pups were still young, and she had fed them as best she could. But now that spring had descended on the Rockies, and the creeks were running swiftly, full with the melted snow from above, she was looking forward to days with plentiful food available.

The morning sun slowly made its way into the cave's entrance, and the mother knew it was time for her to forage. She let her pups know they were to stay in the cave. It took several coarse growls, and a few pushes with her nose to get the message through to her firstborn, the stubborn one. But finally, she persuaded him to stay put. In a few weeks she would bring them out and begin the long education that deep down she knew not all of them would live to finish.

The sun hit her back as she trotted from the cave and a cornucopia of smells assailed her. Damp pine needles, the faint scent of a bear and the assorted varieties of mold from tree bark sitting on the forest floor.

She stood still for a moment, sampling the offerings from the air, and then turned south, toward a breeze that carried a touch of something she couldn't quite place.

Her brisk strides took her quickly to the source of the smell. There was wetness primarily, although her primitive brain couldn't compute that a flash flood had washed away part of the hillside. No, all she knew was that water had been plentiful here, and that something was there, something that made her stomach grumble with hunger.

It took her another ten minutes of investigating until she found it. The odor seemed familiar to her. It reminded the coyote of times she heard the strange creatures near the paths at the edge of her range. But this time it seemed different. And then she recognized it.

Blood.

The smell invigorated her, at the same time that the other smell, the one from the creatures, made the hair on her back stand up. She dug with her front paws at the area with the strongest of the scents. The mud yielded easily to her sharp claws, and the odor of blood became richer. She actually tasted the blood and then the adrenaline hit her as she recognized the feel of bone. She dug and unearthed more of the bone and when an especially large section popped free, she clamped down, her brown eyes scanning the tree line for any sign of movement. She bit and pulled, her warm saliva now coating the bone and freed the carcass from the mud and small, tangled branches.

The coyote lifted her head and pulled until she felt something larger break free from the thick mud. The coyote ran, her body alive with the surprise of finding a much bigger meal than she had initially thought. She pulled the body along behind her until she was out and away from the scents that scared her. The coyote found a small grassy hill from which she could surmise anything that decided to approach her.

She swiveled her head and looked at the edge of the forest. There was no sign of anything she needed to fear. Her stomach vibrated with hunger and she thought of her cubs. The sun broke free from the last of the clouds, and the coyote felt its warmth on her back.

And then she lowered her head and began to feed.

3

Off the coast of Ft. Myers, Florida

The Gulf of Mexico was strangely calm. It was well past noon and the sky was clear with a blazing yellow sun that unleashed the kind of merciless insistence that simply could not be ignored.

Wallace Mack stood in the back of his fishing boat watching the shadows in the water with great interest. He'd been out on the water now for nearly six hours and had already caught some snook but not any of the yellow fin tuna that were his targeted prey.

He reeled in his lure, went to the Yeti cooler and pulled out a cold beer. He moved to the captain's bench under the canopy that provided the only shade on the boat. He took a long drink of the beer and smacked his lips.

He'd lived in Florida now for nearly five years, having spent the majority of his previous twenty-five years in Quantico, Virginia working for the FBI. Virginia was warm for a good part of the year, but nothing like southern Florida. The sun in Florida was a microwave and you could feel your skin cooking by the minute.

But Mack wouldn't trade Florida for anything. He loved it here.

Mack drank from his beer and tried to figure out how much longer he would keep fishing. It was only going to get hotter as the day wore on, and something told him that even though the tide was still up, the peak feeding time had passed. He sipped from his beer and looked out over the flat, jade water. A pelican flew in from overhead and dove not far from the boat.

Mack took that as a good sign.

He drank the rest of beer, went to the side of the boat and cast his lure out.

There were a lot of shadows in the water now; drawn by the two handfuls of minnows he'd tossed into the water. Along with the chum he'd throw into the clear blue water, something was bound to inspire the shadows into action.

His target could smell the blood from the cut bait, and was attracted by the panicked baitfish, struggling to survive.

Mack closed the bail of his reel once he figured his lure had reached the depth he wanted, and began to reel the line in with a start-and-stop rhythm designed to–

The fish hit with a stunning ferocity and Mack reefed on the line, setting the hook, and listened as the fish began to take line out with a fury. The line ripped off his reel and sizzled as it shot out toward the water. Mack estimated at least a hundred yards was taken out before he sensed the fish begin to slow down.

Mack still marveled over the power of the strike. It reminded him of his days playing high school baseball and connecting with a fast ball, the incredibly satisfying thud of power that reverberated through his body.

Now, the line was definitely slowing down so Mack raised the tip of the rod and started to reel it back in, straining against the strength and weight of the fish.

The Gulf of Mexico held a stunning array of species. It was one of the things Mack loved about the fishing in Florida. You never knew what you were going to get. He'd caught everything from snapper, snook and redfish to sea trout, shark and grouper. But judging by the speed and power of the fish at the other end of the line, Mack felt confident it was the tuna he was after.

It took nearly ten minutes for Mack to get his quarry near the boat. The fish must not have liked what he saw because it took off again, this time stripping off another fifty yards of line and bending Mack's rod nearly in half.

The return battle went faster as the fish tired, and soon, he was in sight of the boat.

Mack saw the silvery blue green of the fish and instantly confirmed it was a tuna. The kind that you could put right on the grill and with a little lemon would taste out of this world.

Mack pulled the fish toward the boat, saw the dark shadow, bigger than the others, rise up from the depths and speed like a missile toward the tuna.

Mack grit his teeth. He knew what was coming.

The long dark shadow was without a doubt a bull shark.

Or, as the local fishermen liked to call it, The Man in the Gray Suit.

Bull sharks were attracted by the struggling fish hooked by anglers, and loved to come in and take a big chunk out of the prize, if not the whole thing.

With the risk of breaking his line, Mack heaved as hard as he could on the pole, pulling the tuna toward the boat, trying to make the shark miss even though he was risking a line break.

The gamble worked, but only partially as the shark still got a glancing strike in against the tuna.

Mack felt a brief, violent pull on the line, and then the fish was free and he hoisted it into the boat.

The fish landed on the deck, part of its tail gone, a chunk of its belly missing, and a series of lacerations along its side, spilling blood on the white deck. The tuna was a beauty, the perfect size for Mack at around ten pounds.

He looked again at the bite marks along the side of the fish.

Mack had won, but the shark had levied his tax.

It was a truism among fishermen in the Gulf.

You could catch a lot of fish out here, but sooner or later, you had to pay The Man in the Gray Suit.

4

It didn't take long for Molly Spencer to realize her daughter was missing. To be exact, it was the time it took her to work her way through the two clearance racks at the back of the Nordstrom department store in Des Moines' best shopping district.

Molly's fifteen-year-old daughter Rebecca had told her mother she was going to look for shoes. Molly had said she'd meet her there after she'd gone through the stuff on sale. There had really been nothing there, a cute pressed cotton jacket with a row of beads down the sleeve, but after she thought about it, Molly knew Rebecca would think the beads made the jacket too "little kid-ish." Her daughter was very, very sensitive to anything cutesy.

Molly went down to the ladies shoe department. Even though her daughter was only fifteen, she had good-sized feet. Already a women's size nine.

Rebecca was an athlete, and in her mother's opinion, striking. Blonde hair, blazing blue eyes, and the long willowy limbs of a swimmer, Rebecca turned heads wherever she went. But her daughter was still a very sweet and demure girl. Age-appropriate, her teachers said.

Molly looked for her daughter in the shoe department, but didn't see her. Could she have gone through the entire section already?

A black leather Kenneth Cole slip-on caught Molly's eye and she looked at it. Stylish, but trying too hard. She put the shoe back.

Maybe Rebecca hadn't gotten to the shoes yet. Molly left and walked through the perfume and jewelry areas, back up to the clothes, and then back down to the shoes.

That was about when the general sense of rising anxiety metastasized into the first tingles of fear.

She took out her cell phone to call Rebecca, who had just gotten her own cell phone six months ago, after nearly a year of consistent campaigning. Molly thought about texting her daughter, but then felt a sudden burst of urgency in her stomach, and pressed the contact icon for Rebecca's phone.

By the time it went to voicemail, Molly was scared.

She walked quickly through the entire store, dialing and disconnecting, dialing and disconnecting. She gritted her teeth. Alternately scared and angry, then angry and scared. The two emotions battled for supremacy.

Maybe she was in a dressing room and there wasn't service. Or maybe Rebecca had buried the phone at the bottom of her purse and couldn't hear. It was even possible she'd turned the ringer off, something she had done previously after becoming highly annoyed by her mother's calls.

Finally, Molly saw an information booth just outside the Nordstrom. She walked toward it, and dialed Rebecca's phone again.

As Molly neared the information booth, she saw the woman look up at her as she approached. At the same time, Molly heard an echoing ring, coming just a moment after the one she heard from the earpiece of her own phone.

Molly walked faster toward the information booth and the echoing ring, her heart in her mouth.

The woman behind the information desk looked up as Molly reached her. The woman, who wearing a name badge emblazed with the mall's logo and the name Kate, reached down and picked something up. She held it out toward Molly with a look of confusion in her eyes.

The object in the woman's hand was ringing.

Molly looked at it.

It was her daughter's phone.

5

Locust Springs, Colorado

Locust Springs Deputy Sheriff Windsor Smith felt the pastrami on pumpernickel sandwich from Janet's Deli surge toward his mouth. He turned away from the sight in front of him, staggered a few steps into a patch of long meadow grass, and parted ways with Janet's Wednesday Special.

He wiped his mouth with his sleeve and walked unsteadily back to the scene that had prompted the call from the hikers to the local police.

Deputy Smith had seen bodies before. The first one had been at a seminar on autopsies in Denver, where he'd ended up sleeping with the instructor, a hot forensics expert from Los Angeles with tan skin and jumbo knockers. Actually, he'd ended up studying her body much more than the one she'd dissected in class.

The other dead body he'd seen was a vagrant who'd fallen asleep on the railroad tracks and had been splattered a hundred feet in every good goddamned direction.

But this, this Deputy Smith hadn't been ready for.

First off, it was clearly the remains of a child. The size of the limbs, the shreds of clothing, and a pair of shoes, all made it fairly plain to Deputy Smith that this was a young person.

But there were other things that disturbed Deputy Smith. And even though he had flunked the final sheriff's exam three times before passing, and had barley survived the academy's classes, he was confident enough with his intellect to determine a few things.

Animals had clearly gotten to the body. Things were chewed, and shredded, and pulled apart. There were coyote tracks around the body, a few bird tracks, probably eagles, and smaller prints of maybe a fox or two.

But the body was broken. That was the best way Deputy Smith could put it. Limbs were snapped. The neck, or what was left of it, looked like it was cracked in a ninety-degree break.

Smith turned away again from the scene and looked out over the sloping valley toward the mountains beyond. The air was crisp and clean, and he breathed deeply of the pure stuff, trying to rid his mind of the images.

Still, he was here to do a job, and he tried to focus on what he'd seen, without noticing the gore.

Even though the skull was intact, Smith was pretty sure several teeth were missing from the remains. He was fairly confident in his assessment that the child had been severely beaten. Maybe some of it happened from the animals, and maybe even the elements had caused some damage. But the other condition issues were hard to explain.

Smith didn't know the technical details that would probably make figuring out exactly what happened here a little bit easier. Maybe he would have if he had listened to the forensic expert at the seminar instead of fantasizing about her melons.

But the last detail, well, that was obvious even to him.

The body was more or less intact, with two legs, each having feet attached in little black Nike tennis shoes.

But another item, nearly twenty feet back, sticking partially from the ground couldn't be denied.

It was a child's leg.

This foot, however, was encased in a pink sandal.

Smith closed his eyes and felt the rest of his sandwich start to break for the surface as he realized what this meant.

There was at least one more body.

6

Washington, D.C.

Everything about him was ordinary.

His clothes.

His looks.

His speech.

Even his meal, in this case a Turkey and Swiss sandwich hold the pickle, with a bag of baked potato chips and a Diet Coke.

He sat at a small table by the window with his meal in front of him and his phone off to the left. But he wasn't interested in his phone, or his meal. He only put his phone on the table because nearly everyone else who ate alone made themselves busy with a phone. It was their way of saying that even though they were eating by themselves, they had a very busy, active life, as represented by the energetic use of the phone.

He was also oblivious to the food on the table in front of him. He would probably eat a little just for appearance sake, but ordinarily he would never eat in a place like this.

What did hold a great amount of interest for him, however, was the building across the street.

The one bearing the name of J. Edgar Hoover.

If ever a building represented the activities taking place inside it, the FBI building was it. Huge, faceless, ugly, and intrusive.

The Washington streets were busy around him with office workers scurrying to and from their places of employment. Seeking nourishment in the form of restaurant fare, or a breath of fresh air before returning to their stale offices with bad lighting and nonstop noise.

The man finally deigned to take a bite of his sandwich and chewed, added a potato chip, and washed it down with a sip of Diet Coke.

It was a mechanical process and the man barely registered any flavor in the food he consumed.

Although it was nice enough outside, he had never felt entirely comfortable out of doors. He supposed it had to do with vulnerability, but his preferred locale was in his home office, behind a bank of computers.

Across the street, a panel van pulled up to the gate of the FBI building. Inside the security booth, someone leaned out and accepted the driver's credentials. Moments later, that person handed the items back to the driver and the van pulled into the parking structure of the massive building.

The man in the deli continued to watch, occasionally munching on a chip and taking a sip of Diet Coke.

He wished he had something better to eat, because he was hungry. His workout this morning had been intense, and he had nothing for breakfast but a protein shake. This lunch would not satisfy him.

Then again, he was never satisfied.

The closest he'd ever come to being truly satisfied was

during the six months he'd recently spent in Thailand. It had been an intoxicating time as his dark obsessions grew and blossomed, along with the ease of being able to slake those thirsts.

You could buy anything, or anyone, in Thailand.

And he had.

Nothing was off-limits over there, and everything was available if you had the money. Thankfully, he had plenty of money, and plenty of ideas. It had been fascinating to occasionally watch from outside of himself, as his creativity grew and his appetite for sexual perversion increased exponentially. It was as if his true self had been dormant and the climate in Thailand had brought it out of hibernation.

But the sense that his dark thirsts had been fully satisfied did not last long. As soon as was on a plane back to the U.S. he'd felt that gnawing restlessness that never went away.

Although he didn't clearly articulate it in his thoughts, a part of him understood that sex was vital to his being. The darker and more disturbing it was, the more he enjoyed it.

But he was a man of many hungers.

And it had been on that plane ride back that he first had an idea that rocked him to his core. An idea that combined his one great need, sex, with one of his most powerful, and unfulfilled, quests.

Now, he looked up again at the J. Edgar Hoover building.

He felt himself getting aroused and his face betrayed him by allowing a small smile.

This was going to be one of his greatest endeavors, one that combined both of his most cherished passions.

Sex.

And revenge.

7

Des Moines, Iowa

The tears came and went. And then they came and
went again. And again.

Molly Spencer could not grasp the idea that
Rebecca was gone. Every young woman's voice she heard
sounded like Rebecca's. Every laugh. Every shout. Every cell
phone ring, Molly thought might be her daughter.

But it never was.

As the Des Moines cops talked to her about what had
happened, she kept looking over their shoulders every time
a young girl with dark hair walked past. Each time, she felt a
knife stab her in the heart when the face she saw in no way
resembled Rebecca's.

The police were trying to help. A stocky detective in an
ugly blue suit had been dispatched once they'd heard her
last name. But just like the patrol officers who had first
responded, he had also given her the twenty-four-hour
speech, about how they really couldn't start expending

resources until then. After all, they said, Rebecca could have just gone off with friends or something.

But Molly knew that wasn't true. She knew it in the deepest, truest chords of her heart. Rebecca was her first child, the oldest, and was born with an innate sense of responsibility. Even when she was a little girl, if Molly told her to go to bed at eight o'clock, Rebecca would go to bed at that time, no questions asked. Which isn't to say that she was a patsy. No, Rebecca was a strong, intelligent, independent girl. But she was conscientious and there was no way on God's green Earth that she would have just left the mall without saying a word to her mother. No way. No how. Never.

Molly had immediately called her husband, and he was on his way. Things would happen once Archibald Spencer arrived, Molly knew. He was that kind of man.

But until he got here, Molly was alone. And as the tears burst from her eyes again, she came face to face with what she knew was the absolute, undeniable truth.

Rebecca had been taken.

STOCKING THE SHELVES

8

Silicon Valley, California

It was good to be the boss. He'd finished his last meeting of the day, and it wasn't even five o'clock. But he'd told his secretary to hold all of his calls, went in and shut and locked the door to his office, poured himself some scotch in the thick, square glass that was his favorite. It was actually a double, but because the glass was so big, and made of such heavy leaded glass, it looked like a normal drink.

And then he fired up his computer.

His name was Bernard Evans and his company was called Burn. He'd started the company in his efficiency apartment in Westwood with nothing but some used computers linked together with Kleenex and spit, and built it into one of the most innovative, and profitable, tech companies in the world. Burn specialized in the development and implementation of applications, or apps, primarily for the financial industry.

The company had done quite well, and now Bernard

Evans was worth nearly a billion dollars. In fact, he had slowly been extricating himself from the day-to-day operations of Burn, and turning them over to his protégé, Reese Stocker. Stocker was incredibly bright, but he didn't have Evans' creativity. Which was perfect, because all of the ideas were in place, now it was a matter of just keeping the machine running, and Stocker was perfect for that.

And although Evans himself had the intelligence and experience to develop a bulletproof security system for his own computer, he had hired an outside consultant to set up his personal Internet usage at the office. He had a different IT department that monitored his employees, but his system was totally separate. After the consultant had put the basics in place, Evans rewrote the code for all of the access doors so that only he had access. And then he put in a whole slew of extras that made his online presence completely invisible. But more importantly, untraceable.

He took a long drink of the scotch, felt its warm waterfall of pleasantness tumble through his soul. Christ, he loved good scotch. He caught his reflection in the wall of glass that provided his view of the Pacific Ocean and part of the Santa Monica mountains. Wavy salt-and-pepper hair, an angular face and pale blue eyes. He looked like the wealthy tech exec he really was.

Evans' computer finished firing up and when he saw the screen, his heart jumped a beat.

The icon was staring back at him.

It was animated with photo realistic quality: a young, scantily clad woman walking across his computer screen holding up a sign like the women between rounds of a boxing match. The sign read: OPEN FOR BUSINESS.

Evans felt an immediate stirring in his loins as hot blood coursed through his body. He stood, took his glass, drained it, and refilled it. He walked around his office, trying to get in control, torn between wallowing in the pleasure to come, and wanting to have some control. Gratification was always more powerful after it had been repeatedly delayed. Wasn't it Freud who said that? Evans wondered.

When he felt he'd proven some restraint, he sat back down and clicked on the woman.

And went breathless as the swirling desire of his deepest fantasies suddenly came to life.

9

Des Moines, Iowa

The Spencer home sat high on a hill overlooking Des Moines. It was a sprawling Tudor made of stone and wood, with immaculate landscaping and a wide, expansive yard. The estate bespoke of wealth, power and influence.

In the circular driveway, two patrol cars sat with their engines idling, while two unmarked Crown Victorias were parked along the street.

The police cars bookended a black limousine that was double parked in front of a towering wooden front door that featured black, wrought iron hardware.

Inside the home, there were detectives from the Des Moines police department, FBI agents from the Bureau's office in Omaha, Nebraska. Their office's jurisdiction included Iowa, and several members of Senator Archibald Spencer's team.

The Senator stood in the middle of the great room, his

suit jacket off, his white shirt unbuttoned at the collar and his sleeves rolled up.

"I goddamn know about the twenty-four-hour rule as much as you do," he barked at the lead FBI agent who had just mentioned the need to find Rebecca within twenty-four hours. "Don't fucking tell me about that shit. Fucking find her."

Archibald Spencer was a man of angles. He had broad shoulders that were so perfectly square his fraternity brothers used to joke that he would make a perfect coat hanger. His thin face was hatchet-like, with broad cheekbones that narrowed to a sharply pointed chin. With his height, at least six inches over six feet, his presence was imposing, and when he wanted it to be, menacing.

The senator looked over at the couch where his wife sat.

Their family doctor had given her a dose of Valium which she'd washed down with a gulp of wine. Now, she was alternating between bouts of sobbing and dazed periods of silence.

The FBI's hostage negotiator had arrived fifteen minutes earlier and now sat on one of the Spencer's dining room chairs that he had turned around to face the living room.

"When do they usually call?" the Senator asked him.

"Usually within hours of the abduction," he said. The negotiator's name was Sherman and he spoke with a steady, even voice. "But no two abductions ever go the same way."

"That's fucking great," Spencer said.

He went into the kitchen, got a glass and poured himself a stiff shot of Irish whiskey. Spencer took the drink, went into his library and shut and locked the door.

From his pocket he took a cell phone, thumbed through his contact list until he found the name he wanted.

He sank into the brown leather chair behind his

immense mahogany desk. He pressed the phone icon on the screen and put it to his ear.

While it rang, he looked at the wall of photos opposite his desk. Presidents, politicians, celebrities.

None of them could help him now, the useless bastards.

Spencer knew the fucking twenty-four-hour rule, all right. That something like eighty percent of all child abductions ended with the victim killed in the first twenty-four hours. He thought he'd read that it was actually far worse. That something like seventy-five percent of abducted kids are killed within *three* hours of their capture.

For that reason, he needed someone who could work fast and smart.

Someone who was the absolute best at this sort of thing. And someone he knew personally.

A voice on the other end of the line spoke.

Spencer let out a long breath.

"Mack, it's me," he said.

10

Mack steered the boat into the hoist's cradle, shifted the engine into neutral and shut it off. He caught the nearest post with his right hand to hold the boat steady and then thumbed the power button to raise the hoist.

The hoist locked into place and Mack hooked up the freshwater hose to the engine to clean out the saltwater, drained the livewells and lifted the coolers from the boat and placed them onto the dock. He clambered out of the boat onto the dock, and slid the cooler with the fish over to the cleaning shelf. He quickly filleted the tuna, rinsed everything off and fed the scraps to a pelican who had flown in, landed, and was waiting patiently in the middle of the river. Mack put the filleted tuna back in the cooler and carried the cooler to the house.

Mack's home was quintessential Florida – a three-story structure with the first level being primarily the pool, garage, an outdoor kitchen and a sitting area. The second floor was the main living space, with a wide open lanai that offered sweeping views of the Estero River.

The outdoor areas of the first and second level were screened in and there was many a night when Mack sat on the second floor lanai, overlooking the river, with a beer in hand. He loved to listen to the river as it gently made its way out to the Gulf.

The third floor was Mack's private sanctuary. It included his bedroom, bath, and home office. The home office was where he spent most of his time, reading various law enforcement blogs, news websites, and exchanging email with some of his former colleagues, most of whom were still with the Bureau.

Now, he went to the outdoor kitchen, rinsed the tuna again, placed it on a platter with plastic wrap, and put it in the fridge.

He used the small bathroom off the pool, washed his hands, went back outside, dumped the ice from the fish cooler, and overturned it next to the steps that led to the dock.

Back on the dock, he opened the beer cooler and looked inside. He had three bottles left.

He dragged the cooler over to the simple wooden bench at the end of his dock. The dock itself was a T with the base of the T being the walkway back to the house. The bench sat on the right side of the dock, with a clear view of the river, and the sanctuary on the other side of the water.

Mack pulled one of the beers from the ice, twisted off the cap, and closed the lid of the cooler. He sat on the bench, drained half of the beer in one long pull and smacked his lips.

The river was high, but the tide had started to go back

out, and Mack listened as a soft breeze stirred the palmettos behind him.

He finished the beer, grabbed another from the cooler and saw an osprey fly along the river before landing in a towering tree across from him. The tree was dead, its long branches spread out like fingers on a hand, perfect fishing spots for the osprey.

"Who are you?" a voice said.

Mack turned and saw his sister watching him from the end of the dock. She was tall and thin, and in some ways looked very much like Mack. But a much older, and much more tired version. Now, she didn't look scared, she just seemed curious.

"Hi Janice, it's me, Wallace. Your brother."

Her eyes seemed to flutter as hints of recognition struggled to connect. Mack was never sure just how much registered with Janice, or how much didn't. She suffered from Wernicke-Korsakoff Syndrome brought on by years of severe alcoholism. The condition, known in politically incorrect circles as 'wet brain' had left his sister with a collection of ever-changing psychological maladies that included memory loss, hallucinations and general confusion.

"Oh," she said. "Why are you sitting out here?"

"I just got back from fishing. What have you been up to?"

"I've been painting with Adelia," she said. Adelia was Janice's live-in nurse, a no-nonsense woman who was as good for Mack as she was for Janice.

Mack had noticed the paint on Janice's fingertips. It was an activity his sister enjoyed, but it was also excellent therapy. Anything to challenge the brain, make it connect its circuits. The theory being that one day, if enough connections were made, healing would take place. Janice enjoyed painting with Adelia, but the connections, and the healing, hadn't happened yet.

Janice turned on her heel as Mack's cell phone rang.

He slid the last beer from the cooler, and looked at the caller.

Archibald Spencer.

---

11

100 miles west of Iowa

Rebecca Spencer opened her eyes and saw a sheet of white metal. It took her a moment to realize that she was looking at the ceiling of a van. And that she was inside the van, and it was moving.

Her other senses quickly sent other messages flooding in. Her head hurt. Her mouth was horribly dry. Her body ached.

Worst of all, she couldn't move because her hands were tied behind her back, and her feet were tied together.

The van occasionally bounced and jostled, but the movements were slight. But she could sense the momentum. The sound of an engine running at an even pitch. Rebecca guessed they were driving on a somewhat smooth, and fast surface, probably a freeway. The sense of touch came over her and she could feel the ropes binding her wrists beneath her, and the tightness of tape across her mouth.

And then fear. It came like a great wave of cold water that splashed over her soul, and shook her to the spine.

She closed her eyes as the tears came.

Rebecca saw herself in the restroom at the mall. She had been sitting on the toilet in the stall, texting her friend while she relieved herself. When she was done, she'd gone to the sink to wash her hands. She'd set her phone down, and then she'd knocked the phone through the hole in the counter that led to a wastebasket. She had cursed herself, finished drying her hands and was about to dig through the waste-basket for her phone when someone grabbed her and slapped something across her mouth.

She remembered a chemical smell.

And then there was nothing.

And now this.

Who had taken her and why?

She thought maybe it was a practical joke, but then quickly realized that no one would play a joke like this on her.

No, this was real.

Someone was taking her somewhere.

Rebecca tried to calm herself. It all had to have something to do with her father. He was a Senator and she knew that he had a lot of enemies. He had a lot of friends, too, but there had been plenty of hate mail that reached their house. Phone calls that were somehow made even though their phone number was unlisted, all with messages that in no uncertain terms expressed a severe dislike for Archibald Spencer and his policies.

But what if it wasn't about her Dad?

She squeezed her eyes shut even harder. What if it was some kidnapper rapist who just wanted to take her somewhere and do awful things to her and kill her? Then dump her body in a ditch somewhere?

Rebecca closed her eyes and thought of church. They went pretty much every Sunday to St. Paul's just down the street. It was a beautiful church and Rebecca enjoyed going even though sometimes she pretended to have too much homework to get out of going to Mass.

Now, she pictured the church, the priest, and the feeling of holding her mother's hand during the ceremony. She heard the sound of the church choir singing praise.

Rebecca prayed like she had never prayed before.

And then she started crying again.

12

Silicon Valley, California

Bernard Evans nearly gasped.

The newest product on The Store immediately spoke to him. It was the kind of girl he always looked for as he endlessly surfed through porn sites and triple xxx videos.

A farm girl. Pale white skin. Blonde hair. Blue eyes. Rosy cheeks. Solid and wholesome with meat on her bones and the kind of sweet body you could rock all night long.

And young.

So young she was probably illegal.

He laughed. *This whole thing* was about as illegal as you could get.

He couldn't believe it. For years he'd sought out escorts, street prostitutes, strippers, and worst of all, ordinary women on dating websites just to find his farm girl.

There had always been so much disappointment. The women were either lying online, or using fake pictures, or just somehow never lived up to his expectations.

But this, this was different.

Evans instinctively knew that this girl was the real thing. An honest-to-goodness young, virginal farm girl with flawless skin and a succulence that only came from fresh air and unspoiled innocence.

Now, at long last, here she was.

With a price tag of two million dollars.

Evans smiled. Two million dollars was chump change. Especially considering what he would get for his money. A long weekend alone with this girl in a remote location where he could do whatever he wanted, with no fear of being caught and arrested. His brilliant but clueless partner, Reese Stocker, could manage the day-to-day activities of Burn while he was away.

All of his rape fantasies, his darkest dreams of screwing an innocent young girl literally to death could all come true. He would be completely alone with this girl and free to do whatever he wanted to do to her.

At this price, it was the steal of the century.

Evans was tempted to click the buy button, but he didn't want to rush it. He stood, not an easy task considering the mega erection he was sporting, and crossed the room to refill his glass of scotch. He swirled the amber goodness around the heavy crystal glass and gulped it.

The fire from the liquor warmed his belly, and it matched the heat in his crotch.

He topped off the glass again, then sat back down in front of his computer.

The truth was, he loved this part, almost as much as the rest of it. The waiting, the tension, the possibility that one of the other "customers" would take his dream girl off the site by purchasing her, made it all so tantalizing.

Sometimes, he waited a long time.

Tonight, though, this was different.

He didn't want to risk losing her.

Evans stared at the picture of the girl. His breath became shallow and a flood of images washed over him.

He clicked the button.

And bought her.

And then he had an orgasm that shook him to the core and nearly rocked him from his chair.

13

Locust Springs, Colorado

Still reeling from the information in front of him, Locust Springs Deputy Sheriff Windsor Smith fired up his cell phone.

The phrase "call in the FBI" seemed like something out of a bad movie with Bruce Willis. Die Hard 16, or something like that. Never in a million years would he, Windsor Smith, have thought that one day he'd be picking up the phone calling the number for the FBI in the official Locust Springs Police Department handbook.

But he had no choice.

He had already called in the coroner and his team, as well as some other local law enforcement to help seal off the crime scene.

And then he had gotten honest with himself. He knew that in most cases, local cops resented the Feds. They stonewalled them, wanting to work the case themselves and then bask in the glory of catching a killer.

But Windsor Smith was different. He enjoyed keeping

the peace. Running an orderly operation in his territory. However, when it came to innocent little children being butchered and stuffed into the ground, the whole world went sideways on him. The thought of becoming engrossed in the case disturbed him on a level so deep he could barely register it. Yes, he wanted justice for these little kids, but he was not the man to deliver it. He would help in any way he could, but there was someone else who could do this job much better than he could, and he was either modest enough, or was devoid of the required confidence, that he had no problem admitting it.

Now, with the images of the bodies in the woods, the sight of dead children still rattling his mind, he began to punch in the numbers on his phone with a slightly shaking hand.

How old was this handbook anyway, Smith thought. Were these phone numbers still good? It would be just his luck that the number was out of service and he took forever to somehow get in touch with the FBI. If they never caught the killer, years from now people would look back and say, well, if that local cop hadn't taken so goddamn long to call the Feds.

Smith heard a ring on the other end of the line and then a voice answered, "Denver FBI, how may I direct your call?"

For just a moment, he was at a complete loss for words. Even though it was only the receptionist, Smith struggled to get the words out of his mouth.

Finally, after a quick gulp of lukewarm coffee, and trying not to sound like an overly dramatic bumpkin from the Colorado boonies, Smith eventually told the right person just what he'd found.

14

Federal Bureau of Investigation, Denver, Colorado

If it were possible for shaken nerves to transmit themselves through the phone lines, clear evidence of the phenomenon could have been documented via the phone call from Deputy Sheriff Windsor Smith to Denver Special Agent In Charge Brent Kunzelman.

Kunzelman was a thin reed of a man with thick black hair and long, thin limbs. He looked like a praying mantis in a dark suit. He was also a year from retirement, anxiously awaiting his pension, and looking forward to moving to Montana and memorizing every pool and eddy on the Bozeman River where a lunker trout might be hiding.

The news he got from the local cop didn't exactly make him shake with anxiety, but his blood pressure gained twenty points by the time he was done with the call.

An FBI agent for nearly twenty-five years, Kunzelman had not, by any means, seen it all. A handful of murders, sure, but mostly drug dealing and stupid criminals.

But this was the kind of case he had never expected to pop up in his backyard.

Fifteen years ago there had been a child murdered, but it had been an accident. A shootout between drug dealers and an errant bullet had caught a child sleeping in his bedroom.

But this. Several children, buried in a remote location, with all the signs of mass murder?

The first thing to do would be to visit the crime scene, along with a team of agents, each with a unique skill set. Kunzelman would assign the team, send them on their way, and then he would join them as soon as possible.

Kunzelman was also enough of a veteran to know that this kind of case would need to be reported sooner than later to the head office in D.C.

If there was no immediate evidence pointing them in a clear direction, and he highly doubted there would be, some more investigative assistance would be needed.

Not that he didn't feel he had a world-class group of agents working underneath him, because he did. They had handled everything the world had thrown at them since he was in charge of the office.

To be safe, and if FBI bureaucracy had taught him anything, it was that there was safety in protocol.

So Kunzelman fired up his company laptop, opened his encrypted email program, and began writing an email to his superior in Washington, detailing what little he knew, but at least putting the incident on his boss's radar.

When he was done, he dragged the sent email into a folder he had created within the program.

It was called CYA for Cover Your Ass.

15

Des Moines, Iowa

Mack knew firsthand that when Archibald Spencer wanted something done, it tended to get done, and fast.

Which is why in less than eight hours from the Senator's call to Mack, Mack had packed a bag, been whisked to the Ft. Myers airport, flown to Des Moines first-class, and then promptly transported via black limo to the Spencer home.

The door opened before Mack's driver knocked and Mack saw his old friend looking like he'd never seen him.

"Mack," Archibald Spencer said. Mack took in the tired face, the dark circles underneath the eyes, and the stooped shoulders. But there was still fire in the senator's eyes, and Mack knew that Archibald Spencer would never stop fighting.

"Arch," Mack responded. He and his old college roommate hugged, and then Mack was led into the dining room where a massive oak table had been transformed into a communications center.

Several cops, detectives, and assorted security personnel were milling about.

"How's Molly holding up?" Mack asked. He looked around the cavernous home, not surprised by what he was seeing. Mack hadn't seen Spencer in over five years, and he had never been to his home. Most of their dealings had been in Washington, D.C. when Mack was still on active duty with the Bureau.

"She's sleeping," Spencer said. "With a little chemical help. She's been through the ringer."

"I wish I was here for any other reason," Mack said.

Spencer nodded and then led Mack to an agent. Mack knew that because it was a kidnapping and Spencer was technically a federal employee, the FBI would take control of the case as it fell legally in their jurisdiction.

"Mack, this is Agent Bullock," the Senator said.

Bullock was a short, square man with dark skin and light blue eyes. "Mr. Mack, it's good to meet you."

Mack shook his hand. "Thanks. I don't intend to interfere..."

"Bullshit," Spencer said. He looked at Bullock. "Give Mack everything you have and keep him informed."

That was the Archibald Spencer who Mack knew. Tough, sometimes abrasive, and uncompromising.

"Yes, sir," Bullock said.

"I'm going to check on Molly," Spencer said. He left the room and a tension that Mack hadn't sensed before now seemed to ease from the space along with Spencer's departure.

Mack turned back to Agent Bullock. "Sorry about that, he's in attack mode and I can't blame him."

"I understand," Bullock said. "It's an honor to meet you – I studied a lot of your cases at Quantico."

Mack nodded and changed the subject to Rebecca Spencer. "So what do you have?"

"Not a lot," Bullock admitted. "It was very quick and clean. But we think he got her in the bathroom."

"Security cameras?" Mack asked.

Bullock nodded and motioned Mack over to a desktop computer with a wide screen display. A young man in a wrinkled dress shirt was tapping the keys. He had long, skeletal fingers that flew across the keys faster than Mack could track them.

"Logan, show Mr. Mack the clip."

The young man worked the keys until an image popped onto the monitor. It showed a hallway with a long seating bench, a wastebasket, and a water fountain.

"Check this out," the young man said. He fast forwarded to a specific time at which a young woman entered the ladies room. Logan slowed the video down so Mack could absorb every detail.

"That's Rebecca Spencer," Bullock noted.

Mack watched the girl go into the bathroom. There were no other people in the hallway. Moments later, a janitor rolled a cart into the hallway and then into the ladies room.

"We examined the schedule – the mall's cleaning service wasn't in this part of the mall at the time, and that's not the cart, or the clothing they use," Bullock told Mack.

Mack squinted at the image – it was black-and-white and grainy, but he could make out a relatively short, stocky figure. The face wasn't visible.

In less than a minute, the janitor and the cleaning cart came back out.

"That was quick," Mack said.

"The security camera works on a revolving time schedule," Logan said. "It only captures part of the mall at certain times, so we don't have the actual time it was taken, but it's the same time frame as when we believe the abduction took place."

"And no, Rebecca never came back out," Bullock added.

Mack squinted at the image of the janitor's cart.

Logan must have sensed Mack's focus. "Our best guess is 'Capitol Cleaning Services' and the rest of it is impossible to make out, even with video enhancing," he said. "We've searched and put out the call, but so far, no luck."

"Let me see the whole thing again," Mack said.

He watched the sequence.

"Two things," he said. Bullock took out a notepad and a pen.

"One, that janitor had already picked Rebecca out. It wasn't a case of hitting the bathroom and grabbing whoever might be in there. This was pre-planned. You can even tell that the janitor knows where the security camera is and purposely didn't let it get a good look."

Bullock nodded.

"And the second thing, I'm almost as sure of."

Mack squinted at the computer screen.

"That janitor is a woman."

CUSTOMER SERVICE

16

Nebraska

Her name was Butterfly.

At the same time Mack was studying the security camera footage of her in Des Moines, she was nearly four hundred miles away on the outskirts of North Platte, Nebraska.

It had been a long drive as she had been forced to observe the speed limit for most of the trip. A little extra time was not worth the risk of getting pulled over only to have an overeager traffic cop look inside the van.

Now, she exited the freeway and followed an unpaved road for several miles until she reached the abandoned junkyard. It was a spot she had carefully chosen for its location, and its complete absence of people.

She spotted the pickup truck she had stashed in order to switch vehicles, and saw a man sitting on the ground next to it, with his back against one of the rear tires.

Butterfly didn't hesitate.

She pulled the van up next to the Dodge pickup truck with its camper shell and shut down the engine.

The man watched with silent curiosity as Butterfly got out of the truck.

Finally, he smiled, revealing a row of stained and broken teeth. "Well looky here, my prayers have been answered!"

He got to his feet and Butterfly took in the dirty clothes, the smell of the man, and knew he was a transient who had probably made a temporary home in the back of her getaway vehicle.

"Get away from my truck," Butterfly said.

The man cackled with laughter. "Who the hell you think you're talkin' to little lady?" he said, his voice ragged and raw. "You see any one else out here but you and me?"

He reached into his pocket and pulled out a switchblade. He thumbed a button and the blade shot out with an audible swish.

Butterfly saw the solution instantly and she walked right up to him and with each step that brought her closer his eyes got a little wilder. She could tell he was torn between trying to stab her or running away. She hoped he wouldn't run as her legs were still a little cramped from the drive.

"Get back bitch!" the man hissed.

But by then Butterfly was within an arm's length and he thrust the knife at her. She slapped his arm with her left hand and caught his wrist with her right. She pulled him closer and drove her left elbow into his temple. He sagged and her right hand closed on his wrist. She turned the knife back toward him and slammed it into the center of his chest. He sank to his knees and his hands fell away from his body. Butterfly pulled the knife from his chest and ran its blade across his throat, cutting his neck wide open. He fell to the ground and she thumbed the button on the knife and its blade retracted into the handle. She slipped the knife back into his pants pocket.

Butterfly went to the back of the van, got the girl out, and transferred her to the pickup truck. There was a blanket and a plastic bag of clothes that must have belonged to the homeless man. She took those out.

The truck wasn't as comfortable as the van, but it had a mattress and some tie-downs in the back so she was able to secure the girl in place.

Next, she dragged the dead man to the back of the van and heaved him inside, then did the same with his blanket and clothes bag. She went to the front of the van and wiped it down even though she'd worn gloves, peeled off the Capitol City Cleaners stickers, and tossed them inside the vehicle.

From the back of the van she took a gas can and thoroughly doused the vehicle inside and out, along with the dead man.

It was likely no one would notice the fire, and even less likely that those who did would report it. Smoke at a junkyard? No need to call the police.

Now, she splashed a trail of gas fifty feet away, then tossed a lit match onto the trail.

A bright blue flame erupted and raced to the van.

Butterfly trotted away and climbed into the truck, keyed the ignition, and pulled out of the yard.

By the time the van erupted into flames and exploded, Butterfly was merging onto the freeway, heading for the cabins.

17

Colorado

Charles Starkey was a long way from his plumbing supply business in New Jersey.

But he was alive in a way he'd never felt before.

This was not his first trip to The Store, by any means. He'd performed several transactions already, but each one was special.

This purchase had been no different.

Starkey had been one of the Store's first customers. In what felt like a very brief amount of time, he had spent the vast majority of his wealth on products from this exclusive outlet.

Now, sitting in one of the "kill cabins" as he thought of them, Starkey surveyed the swath of destruction he'd cut in the little cabin's main room. Every muscle in his body, every particle of oxygen in his blood bubbled with a life force he'd never felt before.

But with the smallest hint of disappointment, he realized that the ecstasy he'd felt in the past was fading faster. And each of his purchases had been completed with less time between them. On one level, he realized that it was becoming increasingly difficult to stay satisfied. At the same time, he knew he could never stop.

The boy he purchased two weeks ago was now dead. Starkey had made sure of that.

His victim was facedown on the bearskin rug in front of the fireplace, partially dismembered.

Starkey giggled at the recent memory of his frenzy; he had literally climaxed when he'd felt the boy's death shudder, and he'd begun tearing him apart.

Despite the faint stirring of disgust and regret that always hit him immediately after one of these 'projects,' Starkey felt himself getting aroused again. He checked his watch. They were getting the private plane ready to take him back to New Jersey. His bag was packed, and the limo would be picking him up in ten minutes.

He began to head back toward the boy.

He giggled again.

The more he enjoyed his purchase, the better the value he got for his money.

He figured he had time for a quickie.

18

Des Moines, Iowa

M ack looked across the confined space of Arichbald Spencer's study at Hopestil Fletcher, Deputy Director of the FBI. She had arrived in Des Moines hours earlier and requested an immediate meeting with Mack and Spencer.

Hopestil Fletcher was a tall, imposing woman with broad shoulders, a long angular face, and blazing blue eyes. They had narrowly missed each other at the Bureau, but Mack had heard nothing but good things about her. The word was she was extremely tough but fair.

Now, those eyes were coolly appraising Mack.

"You're going to Colorado," she said.

"Why?" Mack and Spencer simultaneously replied.

Back when he was still with the Bureau, Mack used to accept these assignments with a whirlwind of enthusiasm and questions. And a spine tingling sense of adventure, an eagerness to dive into a case and come out with the solution.

Now, he simply thought about his sister.

Luckily, he knew she would be in good hands with Adelia.

"The local cops pulled three bodies out of the ground in a park 120 miles or so from Denver," Fletcher said. "All of them were children."

"What the hell does that have to do with my daughter?" Spencer asked. Agent Bullock, who had been standing near the entrance to the room, backed away. Smart move, Mack thought. You never want to hear your boss spoken to in a certain way.

"Maybe nothing," Fletcher said.

"Then why are you sending Mack?" Spencer demanded. "I just flew him up here for Christ's sake."

Mack wondered that, too.

Fletcher looked around the room. It was just the three of them now.

"Look, this is highly classified," she said. "But we have been investigating a disturbing pattern of children abductions. The problem is, there is some doubt on whether or not it's a pattern at all. However, some Internet traffic involving two abductions was traced to several broad locations in the West. However, one of them was Colorado."

"So you have a hunch," Mack said. He was a big believer in hunches.

"Not necessarily," Fletcher said. "But the fact that we have another abduction here that at least initially seems very professional, and the discovery of several deceased children in what may be an area of other abductions, does seem to convey a sense of symmetry."

"I think you're right," Mack said.

"Go to Denver. Meet with SAC Kunzelman, he's expecting you," Fletcher said. "They are already investigating so by the time you get there you should be able to make a quick assessment of the situation. Report back to me right away, and then I'll probably have you come right back. You could be back in Iowa in 48 hours.

"Arch?" Mack asked his friend.

Spencer nodded. "If whatever's out there has anything to do with Rebecca, you might be more valuable working that end of this situation."

Fletcher turned to Mack. "Report back to me the minute you have some conclusions. I'll be here with the Senator, he'll be in good hands."

"Got it," Mack said. Fletcher's phone rang and she reached for it. Mack stuck out his hand and Spencer took it.

"Hang in there," Mack said. "We'll find her."

Spencer nodded.

"Damn right we will," the Senator said. "Do what you have to do, Mack, then get your ass back here."

19

Denver, Colorado

Mack thought they should change the nickname for Denver from the "Mile High City" to "Miles from the Airport." It took nearly forty-five minutes for Mack to get from the airport to the city.

He had been to Denver several times and always enjoyed the sight of the city, with its postcard-quality setting in front of snow-capped mountains.

Mack looked at his cell phone. He had debated calling Fletcher, but he had thought about it on the flight and wanted more information on the leads she hinted the Bureau had been investigating.

He felt a little blind going into the situation.

The FBI offices in Denver were on Stout Street and Mack quickly found the building, showed his identification, and was whisked up to a large conference room on the second floor with spectacular views of the city and the mountains beyond.

There were more people in the conference room than

Mack had expected. It must be the entire office, he thought. The twenty or so agents sat around the long conference room table or stood by a variety of easel displays with maps and photos of the crime scene.

A few of them turned and looked at him when he was brought in.

A tall man with dark hair approached Mack.

"Mr. Mack?" he asked.

Mack nodded.

"I'm Kunzelman. Glad to have you here," he said. He turned to the group. "Everyone, I'd like to introduce Wallace Mack from D.C. This case is right up his alley, you've probably heard of some of his exploits."

A variety of people nodded at Kunzelman's assumption, others simply stared at Mack. Kunzelman turned back to him.

"Mack, I'm going to have each person who's in charge of a clear aspect of the case to brief you, it should take about two hours. Once you've been briefed, I assume you will want to go to Locust Springs and see the crime scene firsthand."

"Yes, definitely," Mack said.

"Okay, then, folks, let's get this man up to speed."

It took closer to three hours, and by the end, it was clear that they didn't have much to go on.

With his laptop open before him, Mack quickly perused an email with attached documents Director Fletcher had forwarded to him. He had been reading through them as the Denver team briefed him.

Now, they all looked at him, expectant expressions on their faces.

"Who here has some cybercrime expertise?"

It caught them off guard.

Finally Kunzelman said, "Uh, that would be Jerry."

Mack looked around the room but no one reacted.

"Uh, he isn't here. In the room, that is," Kunzelman explained. "I can have you taken down to his office, if you'd like."

"That would be great. And then I'm going to need a car and directions to the crime scene."

Kunzelman nodded, and a young agent took Mack down to the office of Jerry Renfro, a middle-aged man with a handlebar moustache. The younger agent made the introductions, and then Mack opened up his laptop, clicked open the documents Fletcher had sent him, and began asking questions.

20

Washington, D.C.

There were days, and today was one of them, where he felt less like a man with an addiction and more like an addiction that resided in the body of a man.

Everything in his life could be traced to it.

His rotten childhood. His tortured life as a young man. His inability to hold steady work. And his current station in life.

He was Owner of The Murder Store.

And wanted by the FBI.

His name was Terry Piechura and he always wondered if it was his addiction that drove him to develop a genius-level intellect when it came to computers, or if it was his amazing skill in the cyber world that ultimately facilitated his extremely divergent sexual compulsions.

It didn't matter, of course. What did matter was that as a tertiary supplier to a non-classified government entity, he had hacked his way into the national criminal database and had expunged his name from every law enforcement computer in the country.

This allowed him to get his passport and travel to the Far East for his hobby.

Ultimately, however, he had left a breadcrumb or two and that hadn't gone over well with law enforcement.

But he was getting his revenge now.

And boy was he having fun.

Piechura went into his office and logged into his bank account. He saw that one of his best customers, Bernard Evans, had pulled the trigger on young Rebecca Spencer. The quick photos Butterfly had taken of the girl weren't great, but they had obviously struck a chord with Evans. Piechura smiled. He had seen Evans' name all over the place as a software genius and billionaire. Well, that may have been true, but Piechura knew that Evans had the same kind of interests he had. And satiating those thirsts was an expensive proposition.

The Owner of The Store confirmed the deposit, immediately transferred it through several shell accounts, and then split it into dozens of small amounts, and funneled them separately into his main account in the Bahamas.

He then picked up his satellite phone, punched in the number for the remote router located in his supercomputer in the San Fernando Valley, and placed a call to his associate.

"Hello, Butterfly, my love," he said. "I have your next assignment."

21

Nebraska

Rebecca Spencer was a pendulum. One minute she was terrified, ready to scream and cry at the same time, the next minute she was angry and prepared to fight to the death.

She had been consumed with hope when the van stopped. Her mind went on an image sprint: the driver abandoning the truck, Rebecca hearing the sound of voices. And then she was being dragged from the van.

The first thing she saw was the dead man. There was no doubt he was dead. There was a gaping wound across his throat and his shirt was covered with blood. His face was white and frozen, his eyes wide and staring into nothing.

"What are you doing?" Rebecca screamed at the woman.

The woman ignored her, and pushed her into the truck, and tied her in place.

Minutes later, the smell of gasoline filled the air around her.

An engine started up, and then an explosion, and they were driving once again.

At that point, her hopes had gone up in flames with what she assumed to be the van. Rebecca figured that her captor had probably switched vehicles and for some reason had set the abandoned vehicle on fire. Probably to destroy evidence.

Rebecca thought about the dead man. She had never seen a dead person before, except for her grandmother at a funeral home, and that hadn't even looked like the woman she had known. But now, seeing that dead man who had just been alive moments before? Rebecca wanted to vomit, in fact, she felt the bile rise in her throat but she fought it back down.

Who was this woman? Rebecca thought more and more that her kidnapping might be political. Usually, men kidnap young women to rape and kill them. But this woman had knocked her out in the ladies room at the mall. Which convinced Rebecca that the dead man had probably been an innocent bystander. Unless he had brought the truck so her captor could switch vehicles.

She desperately wished for her mother. For some reason, even though they fought a lot, it was her mother who she couldn't stop thinking about. How much she wanted to hug her Mom and be home in her own bed.

Tears slipped out and ran down her cheeks.

Think, Rebecca, think.

She told herself to stop being such a big baby. In the novels she read, the heroine was always resourceful. Well, she could be resourceful, too.

For instance, she recognized that this vehicle was a lot different than the other one. This one's engine sounded bigger, and the ride was rougher. It was a truck, and a rugged one. Was that a clue to where they might be going?

The window between the cab of the truck and the bed was cracked slightly, probably so the woman could keep an eye on her, but Rebecca was glad, because she felt like she could at least get some idea of what was going on.

For instance, when the phone rang, and she heard the woman's voice, she could tell that the woman sped up almost immediately.

Rebecca wasn't sure if that was a good sign or bad.

At this point, all she could do was hope.

22

Somewhere over the Midwest

I t wasn't until he was on the plane, heading back to New York, that Charles Starkey felt the buzz begin to wear off. At first, he alternated between giddy flash memories of what he'd done to the boy in the cabin, and then he would snap to images of walking in the door of his home.

Back to his wife.

And back to his bank account.

Or what was left of it.

He'd gotten pretty creative with his accounting – transferring balances from the family business to fake suppliers before funneling them into a separate personal account he used for his hobby.

It had taken a long time for him to save the money he had to pay for this latest boy, but he didn't regret it. Not one bit.

Still, when he thought about some of the things he'd done, it made him a little nervous. He owed money, through the business, to some people. The kind of people you didn't want to owe money. And certainly not the kind of people you wanted to be late in paying.

For some reason, they had seated him in an exit row on the plane, and he had the crazy idea to rip open the door and jump out of the goddamn plane.

But he couldn't.

But with each minute he flew back east, it seemed the intoxicating euphoria of what he'd done wore off a little bit more and was replaced by a gnawing fear of what all of this was costing him.

It was bad enough he owed a lot of money to people that he should never associated with in the first place. But he had also drained most of the plumbing business's money to fund his excursions.

Not only would his family be extremely angry with him, but he would probably go to jail for the creative book-keeping he had been employing. Most of what he'd done was highly illegal.

Prison or death?

Those couldn't be his only two options.

He just had to get creative.

And even though he told himself this before, he simply couldn't afford The Store anymore. This boy would be his last.

If he could stop spending money, he could build back up some of the money he had taken. To pay it all back was out of the question, but at least he could hide how much he'd taken.

The key would have to be to control himself.

Something he had not been very good at lately.

What it really came down to was the choice between three things.

Prison.

Death.

Or no more purchases at The Store.

A shadow passed over his soul. A shadow that felt a lot like truth.

23

Locust Springs, Colorado

The forest was empty and cold. Mack felt foolish for not bringing a warmer jacket, even though the FBI agents didn't seem to be bothered by the cold. Then again, he was now a Florida boy. With thin blood that preferred eighty-five degrees and sunny.

Mack looked around the clearing. They were in a shallow, natural draw, surrounded by tall pines, some spruce, and rocky, uneven ground.

Before them was an empty hole. The bodies had been removed and the area was still surrounded with crime scene tape.

Mack stood looking at the dark earth, felt the gray clouds roll in over him. He shrugged his shoulders against the cool, moist air.

"Talk about the middle of nowhere," one of the agents said. Mack knew they weren't sure what to do. After all, the crime scene guys had been here and left, the area thoroughly scoured for any tracks or evidence. They had probably been told to take the former profiler out to the crime scene and stay out of his way.

Mack pictured the map in his head. The location made sense. North and south of Denver was where you would find more cities and a denser concentration of people. Directly west was another bad idea as that's where Interstate 70 ran. So if you were looking to dispose of bodies, you would go either northwest or southwest from Denver. This area was northwest, beyond the Arapaho National Forest, north of I-70, but south of Highway 40.

The middle of nowhere.

"The autopsy will give us some answers," Mack said. "Were they already dead when they were brought here? Had they eaten? If they were already dead how long had they been dead? Maybe then we'll be able to answer some questions."

The agent nodded.

Mack looked at the side of the hill that had washed away in the rain. It was really impressive how much land had given way.

He'd chased enough killers to know that no matter how good they were at planning, there was always the possibility of some unforeseen event that could derail their best-laid plans. In this case, a flash flood.

"It's actually good news," Mack said.

"What's good news?" the agent asked.

"Well, that we found them, certainly. But if you look at the depth of this draw, and how much soil was washed away it tells you that whoever buried these bodies, buried them in much deeper ground than most murderers."

"And that's good news?" the agent said.

"Sure," Mack replied. "Because the deeper and more

permanent a killer buries his victims, the more it means his plan was that they would never be found."

The agent nodded but didn't say anything. Mack could tell he still didn't get it.

"So the good news is that when killers dispose of their victims' bodies in public areas, where they know they'll be found, they're much more likely to try to destroy any evidence," Mack said. "But in cases where they think no one will ever find the body, well, a lot of times they just don't want to take the time to destroy evidence."

The agent nodded.

It was cold enough that Mack's breath hung in the air above him.

"In other words, their confidence leads to them not being as careful as they should have been. Which, sometimes, means they leave evidence."

He thought of his friend Archibald Spencer, and the words of Hopestil Fletcher rang in his ears.

There could be more.

Mack turned his attention to the things he could control and tried not to worry about the rest.

"Let's hope they left something for us to find," Mack said. "And that we find it, fast."

24

Colorado

When the tailgate swung open with an agonizing screech, Rebecca squinted against the small influx of light that made its way into the back of the truck.

She was facing away from the tailgate, and immediately saw just how dirty and disgusting the truck was. There was dirt, rust, and a few strands of what she assumed to be hay. It also smelled vaguely of farm animals.

Rebecca felt the restraints being loosened behind her back, and then she was pulled from the truck.

She came face to face with her captor for just a brief moment. Rebecca got a glimpse of a sharply drawn face, beautiful but severe, with eyes that seemed to look past her.

The woman spun Rebecca around and she felt a hand push her forward and she started walking, stumbling at first, unsure of where she was going with legs that were in dire need of circulation.

The air was cold. Rebecca tried to look but she was being marched quickly toward a small cabin. They were surrounded by trees. Rebecca thought she caught a quick glimpse of mountains beyond.

Rebecca struggled to get her bearings. She had to fight, somehow. And right now all she could use was her mind.

It was fall in Iowa, so she had to be at a higher elevation for it to be this cold, unless the Midwest was experiencing some kind of dramatic cold snap, which she doubted. No, Rebecca figured they had gone west from Iowa, maybe to Colorado, Wyoming or Utah. Maybe even Montana.

Rebecca knew that there were some anti-government people out in the West, although she vaguely recalled them being more in Idaho than anywhere else, but she wasn't sure if that was the case.

So she was probably in one of the Western states where the Rockies were. No matter where it was, she thought, it was a long way from Iowa.

The hand in the back pushed her forward again, and she kept walking straight through the front door of the cabin. The woman reached around her, opened the door, and pushed Rebecca inside.

There was a nearly overwhelming smell of disinfectant that scared the hell out of her.

What had happened here?

Her eyes were just beginning to adjust to the darkness of the cabin's interior when a sharp pain hit her upper arm and she saw that a needle had been jabbed into the meat of her arm.

She struggled, but the woman held her in place, quite easily, Rebecca realized, and everything quickly began to feel thick. Her face, her tongue, her feet.

The cabin went out of focus and she heard a strange wooshing sound in her ears.

And then she felt nothing at all.

SALE OF THE DAY

25

Colorado

On pick-up and delivery days like this, Butterfly often thought she could smell the flames of her home as it burned and her family lay dying. Of course, she couldn't really be sure of what she remembered. She had only been a few years old at the time. Most of what she knew about the horror had been told to her.

Yet none of that knowledge changed the smoldering scent of death that seemed to penetrate her consciousness.

Now, in the cabin, she put the new target on the bed and firmly fastened the restraints.

Butterfly felt nothing inside. Her mind moved in jagged bursts, jerking from one task to the next while her body moved with an unnatural grace. She had always been like this. After her family had died, she had been sent to a home with other children like her.

It was where she had met the only person in the world she loved. He had helped her when no one else could, or would.

For as long as she could remember, she had always been the fastest on the playground and not just among the girls. She could outrun, out jump, and later, out punch any boy she met. Because there had been fights. Violence had proven to be something that she felt comfortable with. It wasn't long before she sought it out with increasing frequency.

They had all feared her. Everyone at the orphanage. The students. And the adults.

But that was all in the past, something she rarely thought about. Only on delivery days.

Now, she knew what she had to do. The lingering scents of death and darkness were always pushed away by his familiar words, the image of his face and the subconscious emotion that he was her only tenuous connection to life itself.

Butterfly shut and locked the cabin and crossed the small compound to the other cabin.

When she opened the door, her eyes took in the carnage before her. She had seen worse.

She bundled the body in a specially made body bag, put it on an ambulance stretcher, and wheeled it out to the truck. She went to the caretaker's cottage, and brought in the cleaning supplies, disinfectant, and bleach.

It took her several hours to restore the cabin to its original state.

When she was finished, Butterfly put the cleaning supplies back in the caretaker's cottage, and then she performed the most important task of the day.

She checked the cabin's hidden cameras via the video control center just off the main room of the caretaker's cottage.

Butterfly sped through the actual footage, not wanting to

watch any of it, and when it reached the end, she saved the file to the computer's hard drive, made a copy, and forwarded it to The Owner.

Almost immediately, her phone rang. And since only one other person possessed the required number, Butterfly knew who it was.

She answered the phone and The Owner gave Butterfly her new set of instructions.

26

Silicon Valley

Bernard Evans had no post-purchase regret.

As much as he enjoyed the shopping aspect of his secret passion, there was no doubt he would make a purchase. It was the thrill of the hunt, with the girl being the trophy, but instead of a gun he used his bank account. Besides, he thought with a smile, an overflowing bank account was much more dangerous than a loaded firearm.

Ordinarily, people who committed money to major purchases often felt a sense of guilt, or even fear, over what they had done. But Evans had no such emotion. The purchase was the climax, the shopping the foreplay.

He imagined it was like an alcoholic who claimed to love the atmosphere of his favorite smoky bar. Who raved about the camaraderie, the banter with the bartender. But he was really there for the booze, for the high it brought, and he could talk all he wanted about the social aspects of the bar, but he went there for one reason only; to get stoned.

And for Bernard Evans, getting stoned was murder.

So he had bought the girl.

It was the most he'd ever spent at The Murder Store, by far. But he knew she would be worth it. He'd been buying what he considered "bargains" up to that point. Women who were drifters, or runaways, some even former prostitutes or escort service types. Strippers down on their luck.

But in the back of his mind, he knew he was getting ready for bigger and better things. He was like the gambler who started at the smaller pot tables, graduating to the big time.

And this girl was the big time.

Wholesome, all-American, from the Midwest. Clean, pure, no tattoos or piercings. She was like the girl next door.

But he, Evans, had never had a girl next door. He'd fucking lived in a trailer park, the only "girls next door" were fifty-year-old waitresses who chain smoked and smelled like dirty locker rooms.

He'd known a few girls in school from time to time, but he'd always been moving, always going to new schools, the perennial new kid who either got beat up or made fun of. He would finally begin to make a place for himself, and then the family would move again.

It was what happened when the authorities were always curious about you.

But he'd never forgotten those women and men at the trailer park smoking cigarettes and drinking, even in the morning.

In fact, sometimes, sitting at the head of a conference table, overseeing a software company takeover, or an IPO that was netting him hundreds of millions of dollars, he swore he could smell the cigarette smoke and spilled Night Train wine on the trailer park's gravel walkways.

No, he was going to have this girl. That was a certainty.

Thanks to The Murder Store.

He figured there were only a few customers. Oh, there were probably plenty who shared in his dark, murderous fantasies. But how many had the money to make it happen?

So he'd put his best efforts to uncover the trail of The Murder Store, for his own security, and he'd never been able to crack the encryption, the switchbacks, the identity screens. And that made him happy.

Because he knew that if he couldn't crack The Murder Store, no one else could, either.

27

Denver, Colorado

The bodies were on the gurneys, centered, with sheets covering them. The sheets and the steel surfaces were much too big for the tiny objects they held.

Their footsteps rang hollow on the tile floor as Mack and the FBI agent assigned to be his escort approached the bodies.

The coroner reached for the sheet covering the first body and Mack held his breath. The coroner's assistant, a young man with a thick beard, stood nearby.

The sheet was pulled away and the first thing Mack saw was the face of a young boy whose eyes were wide open, his skin and features badly decomposed.

But still, Mack could tell the boy was very young and no matter how much death he had seen, Mack felt darkness cross his soul.

The coroner began speaking, but Mack had trouble

following what the man was saying. He felt sick to his stomach and had a moment of lightheadedness.

"Are you all right, sir?" the coroner asked. He was a short, rotund man with a bald head and thick black glasses.

"Yes, please go on," Mack said, his voice unsteady.

The coroner continued his report but Mack could barely hear him.

The phrase "massive trauma" and "torture" were the only things that cut through. The coroner estimated the time of death to be between six to nine months earlier.

He moved on to the other two bodies and Mack blocked everything from his mind.

He realized why he had left the Bureau. He no longer had the courage to face what one human being could do to another. Mack tried to focus on the coroner's face but he felt sweat break out along his forehead and his stomach was queasy. It reminded him of the first autopsy he ever attended, decades ago. Mack actually thought he had been stronger back then.

Not like now.

The mind was like a callus. The more pressure and abrasion, the tougher it became. Too long without it, and the callus grew soft.

Mack was soft now, he knew that.

"Do you have a written report?" Mack asked, interrupting the coroner. The man nodded to his assistant who gave Mack a thick folder.

"Is there contact information for me to call you if I have any questions?" Mack asked.

"It's all in there," the coroner said. Mack sensed irritation in the man's voice.

Mack followed the agent out the parking lot where they

parted ways. He got into his rental car and headed for the general direction of his hotel.

The fresh air had done him some good.

And now, the feeling of sick helplessness was gone.

It had been replaced with anger.

28

For the gazillionth time, Rebecca Spencer's hand reached for the cell phone that she no longer had.

"Stop doing that!" she yelled at herself. Her thin voice echoed in the empty room. Every time she did it, out of habit, it made her want to cry because it slammed home that her life as she had known it was being changed forever.

She didn't have her phone. She didn't have her parents. And she had no real idea where she was. Or who had taken her.

The urge to scream overcame her but she fought it down. She knew there was no one else out there. At least no one who would help her.

It would be wasted effort.

What she did have was a fairly good idea of *why* she'd been taken. Her Dad was a Senator, had a lot of money, and would pay anything to get his daughter back.

For a brief moment, she considered the possibility that it was a political kidnapping. A terrorist act. Rebecca knew that America had a lot of homegrown terrorists and that most of them saw the government as the enemy. An evil empire that had grown too powerful and was going to take away everyone's individual freedoms.

But the more she thought about it, the more she discounted that fact.

It just didn't feel to her like she had been grabbed by some kind of crazy group of political fanatics.

This felt like a very focused, motivated individual.

And her guess was that it was all about money.

So Rebecca had been kidnapped, and she was guessing that a ransom had been demanded.

And she knew her Dad would pay.

She also knew that her father would never rest until he caught the bastards who had taken her.

Rebecca had read plenty of news stories about her Dad, and she knew that he had a reputation for ruthlessness, even among the cutthroat back stabbers of Washington.

Everyone said that she took after him in looks...and disposition.

So Rebecca knew what her parents would say to her. That she needed to do what the kidnappers wanted. Don't cause trouble, they would say to her.

Well fuck that.

Her mouth was still dry and she stunk. The assholes had drugged her!

She wasn't going to play nice.

She was going to fight.

Right then, Rebecca Spencer decided that up until now, her captors had experienced the easy part of their mission.

From here on out, she would make things a lot more difficult for them.

She vowed to make these cocksuckers *earn* their pay.

29

Charles Starkey was having a tough time with the eggs.

This morning, seeing how pale and wan he looked, his wife had ordered him to eat two eggs she made for him. They were accompanied by two slices of toast and a glass of orange juice.

He had choked them down, barely. What he had been unable to do was make any sort of coherent conversation with his wife. He had mumbled, lost his train of thought, broken out into a cold sweat.

Eventually, she suggested he go back to bed as it was obvious he was under the weather.

Instead, he went into his home office, shut the door, and slid the deadbolt.

Now, seated at his desk in his office, the eggs were threatening to come back up and out.

Like everything else he had experienced that moment, he just swallowed it back down.

He spread his hands out on top of his desk and braced himself in his office chair.

For a crazy moment, he felt like the captain of a ship that was veering in all directions and he was powerless to gain control. Starkey laughed at the idea. The sound came out of his mouth less like a chuckle and more like a small dog stifling a bark.

With a feeling like he was disembodied, he raised his hands and watched them tap out the password to his computer.

The screen came to life.

Somehow, he managed to log onto his bank account.

This time, there was no denying what he was up against.

The double whammy walloped him. The first was an up-to-date balance sheet showing last month's profits, all of which had been funneled into a private account for his recreational tryst in the mountains of Colorado.

The second part of the blow was a series of urgent messages sent to his work email, his personal email, and his business cell phone, which he now held in his pale, shaking hand.

He didn't even remember taking it out of his desk drawer.

All of the messages were from some less than desirable "businessmen" associated with Newark's underworld. The emails were coded, but the message was clear.

Starkey's eyes shifted from the balance sheet that seemed to pulsate like a monster's eyeball in a horror film, to the messages.

He couldn't help but notice that the messages had arrived over the course of several days and with each message, the tone had changed. Initially, the communication was clear, but not overtly threatening.

The last message, however, had dropped all pretense.

It had been a simple missive.

Time was up.

Suddenly, Starkey bolted from his chair and rushed to his private bathroom, the eggs charging up toward freedom with astonishing urgency.

He made it just in time.

30

M ack went to his hotel, checked in, unpacked, slipped into a T-shirt and sweatpants and cracked a cold beer from the minibar.

He sat at the desk, put the coroner's report in front of him, and waited until he'd finished his first beer, then poured himself a second, then reached for his cell phone.

He called his home phone in Florida and Adelia answered.

"Hey Adelia, it's me," he said.

"Mr. Mack, how is Iowa?" she asked.

"It was good, but I'm in Colorado now."

"You sure do get around," she said.

Mack could hear the sound of soft reggae music in the background. Both Adelia and Janice loved reggae, and so did Mack. Janice found it especially calming.

"How is she doing?" Mack asked.

"Just fine, just fine," Adelia said. "We spent a long time in the pool today and now she's tired."

As was his habit, Mack fought the urge to ask Adelia to put Janice on the phone. It was pointless. She was only confused by the sound of his voice, especially if she was unable to realize who he was, which was most often the case.

"When are you coming home?" Adelia asked.

Mack looked down at the autopsy reports in front of him. He let out a sigh.

"I'm not sure," he said. "This is a bad one."

Over the years, Adelia had become much more than a caregiver to Janice. She and Mack had become a partnership of sorts, and at this point in his life, she knew him better than anyone else.

It was not a romantic relationship as Adelia was happily married. Besides, Mack was not about to risk losing the best thing that had ever happened to Janice since she'd been diagnosed.

Adelia was, and continued to be, a lifesaver for both of them.

"You do what you have to do, Mr. Mack," she said. "You know I believe you were put on this Earth to do good by stopping those who do bad. So you do your job and come home when you're done. We'll be waiting."

Mack laughed, thanked her, and disconnected the call.

He set his empty beer in the hotel's wastebasket, and got another one out of the fridge.

From his briefcase, he opened his laptop and a new document in which he could type out his notes and thoughts as he went through the reports.

At long last, he couldn't put it off any longer.

He opened the first page of the first report and began to read.

It was worse than he could have imagined.

Ordinarily, it took almost no time for Bernard Evans to pack. He usually threw in a few Hugo Boss shirts, some dress pants, a pair of jeans and he was good to go.

But today was different.

Today, everything took five times longer than usual.

Because this trip had to be perfect.

He had bought the perfect girl and now he wanted everything else to be just as flawless. Plus, he wanted to savor every single moment of this entire experience. It wasn't just about getting his money's worth, although that was a big part of it.

It also gave him ample opportunities to visualize. For instance, his pants. What pair of pants did he want to have on when he had the girl tied up and ready to begin his fun? Which zipper would he pull down so he could–

He stopped himself before he went too far. He didn't have time to jack off right now.

In the end, he took an entire extra suitcase, to give

himself every possible option for his attire. He also threw in some unusual implements that he didn't take on normal business trips.

Bernard Evans drove his Bentley 8 to the private airstrip where a jet was waiting. It wasn't his own aircraft, the one he used for nearly all of his business trips. No, this one had been leased through a shell company and all of the papers were forged with false signature and passenger details. Should the authorities ever try to find his name on any kind of manifest, it would be nowhere to be found.

Even the plane's eventual destination had been doctored. According to the flight plan, a group of three women, executives at a steel manufacturing plant in Pennsylvania were flying to Canada for a company summit.

He laughed. Money could buy anything.

Evans gave his bags to one of the flight personnel who promptly stowed them, and then he climbed on board.

He settled himself into the deeply luxurious leather seat and poured himself a thick glass of scotch. Evans closed his eyes and relaxed. He heard the boarding door close and he took a moment to buckle his seatbelt.

The pilots closed the door to the cockpit.

The plane's engines rose in pitch and they taxied down the runway.

Evans felt his own heart race to match the revving of the engines. They took off and as the jet rose above the California foothills, Evans drank the booze from his glass until it was empty. He quickly poured himself another.

He knew the flight would be short, less than an hour, and that he would land in Colorado. There, he would take a rented car to a second airport, and get picked up by someone from The Store.

Evans stretched his legs out in front of him.
He thought of the beautiful girl from Iowa.
Soon, he thought. *I will see you soon.*

LOYALTY REWARD PROGRAM

32

Butterfly placed the bodies in the back of the truck, drove out the gate, reset the alarm systems, and took off. It would take her six hours to reach the state park just across the border with Wyoming. It would take her another three or four hours to find a spot and bury the bodies, and then another six hours to drive back to the compound.

That would be just in time to prepare for the arrival of the next guest.

She checked the satellite phone on the seat next to her. There were no messages just yet.

She longed to hear his voice, even if it sounded tinny through the extreme security measures she knew he took in his communications.

Her job was lonely, but important.

Butterfly never resented her work.

She did it for *him*, mostly. And for the charred remains of her past.

They had come together in their teens and both recognized the perfection of how they fit. Two puzzle pieces instantly locked together.

It had been murder that brought them to each other. Butterfly's kill, his knowledge of what to do in the aftermath. Both skills came with such a natural ease that neither one of them had to think about what they were doing. They just did it.

She had been in trouble all of her short life, but when the man who ran the orphanage took things too far, she had simply stabbed him to death with a letter opener. She had become curious about killing and so she took her time with him. Dispassionately slicing and probing, judging blood loss.

He had barged in on them. Butterfly remembered looking into his eyes, expecting reproach, but instead saw love and acceptance.

Immediately, he shut and locked the office door. Deleted any trace of them from the computer and stole their files.

From there, they left.

Started a new life together.

He had suggested they pick new names. She watched as he built a computer from scrap parts and began hacking into databases, erasing what they both wanted to destroy and creating a new future for them.

Still, he wanted a name.

It was one of her earliest memories. An island somewhere near a lake with quaint streets and brightly painted houses. A hill with an old church.

And something called a butterfly house.

She remembered going inside, sitting on a bench and watching as hundreds of butterflies floated around her. It was like a cocoon. Beautiful and strange.

Later, when she was forced to do horrible things, she

often retreated into the butterfly room and waited until it was over.

Oh, he gave her a different name for the computer stuff.

But from then on, she was someone totally new and different from anything anyone had ever been before.

Butterfly.

33

M ack didn't have nightmares when he finished reading the autopsy reports on the children's bodies found in the ground in the woods outside Locust Springs.

He didn't have nightmares, because he didn't sleep.

Mack read the coroner's report at least five times, highlighting and rereading certain sections another dozen times. When he at last closed the folder, most of the beer he'd bought at the liquor store down the street was gone. He walked to the hotel room's small loveseat and turned on the television. There was a travel channel, featuring a host with a lisp who was backpacking through Norway.

The light from the television caught his face and he may have slept, or at least faded into unconsciousness and back again. In his near wakefulness state, Mack saw the bodies of the children. He saw the way they had been treated, what had been done to them, and eventually, how they had been killed.

They were horrible crimes.

But what also troubled Mack wasn't the similarities of their deaths, it was the differences.

The nine-year-old girl had been tortured. There were burn marks over most of her body, obviously done in a systematic pattern. And she had died of strangulation.

The ten-year-old boy had been beaten to death. A vicious and thorough punishment that had occurred in a matter of minutes.

The other victim, a seven-year-old girl, had been stabbed to death in a wild frenzy of violence. Nearly all of the wounds had been inflicted post-mortem.

Aside from the cruelty, and the unimaginable pain the victims must have gone through, Mack kept going back to one conclusion, and it was what troubled him so much, knowing what he was up against.

He was certain that all three children had been murdered by different killers.

34

The next morning at Denver FBI headquarters, Mack let SAC Kunzelman begin the meeting with the latest.

"We put a rush on all of the forensics and got a lot of hits. The first victim's identity is Chris Velasquez from Miami, Florida."

Other agents were rapidly pinning information to the victim charts placed around the room.

Victim number two is Emily Lu from San Francisco. Chinatown, to be exact."

"Last seen?" Mack said.

"A sporting goods store."

"Are we getting copies of everything, the detective's reports, witness interviews?" Mack asked.

"It's all on the way," Kunzelman said. "We've also put out a message to all law enforcement agencies, asking about possible recent abductions/missing persons cases."

"There has to be a link somewhere between these kids," Mack said. "There has to be."

"I agree. There has to be a pattern, a reason these kids were selected," Kunzelman said.

Mack looked at the photographs on the wall. He had them seared into his memory, as well as the police reports on the abductions.

"You know, it's interesting," he said, as several random thoughts clicked into place.

"What is?" Kunzelman said.

"Stereotypes."

"Uh-huh."

"If you told me a kid was abducted in Miami, what ethnicity would I think the kid was, based on general statistics?"

Kunzelman thought about it. "Well, I believe Latinos are the majority in Miami, right? So that would be my guess."

"And if a young girl was abducted from a mall in Iowa, what ethnicity would you guess she was?"

"Again, if you were playing the odds, you would say a white girl, a farmer's daughter."

Mack nodded.

"We all know that these days just about every ethnicity is present in every city across the country. But at first, I thought, well, it makes sense that a Latino was taken in Miami, a white girl was taken in Iowa, because statistically, those are the best odds, right?"

Kunzelman nodded. "Statistically speaking, yes."

"Sure, even though I'm sure Des Moines has its ethnic neighborhoods, just like Miami has upscale white neighborhoods, the victims are members of the majority population," Mack said. "Statistically, they would be the ones most likely taken."

Kunzelman waited for the other shoe to drop.

"But what if it's the other way around?" Mack asked.

"What do you mean?" Kunzelman asked as the room fell silent.

Mack gestured at the reports on the wall.

"What if the perp needed a young Latino, so they went to Miami? And then a young Asian girl so they went to Chinatown. And finally, they needed a purebred white girl of solid Midwestern stock, so they went to Des Moines?"

Kunzelman thought about it.

"Someone would have to be giving specific orders to fill. Like car thieves do," he said.

"Exactly," Mack answered. "And the person who took Rebecca Spencer in Des Moines, if her case is related to this one, was a woman. And women are rarely serial killers," Mack said. "Poisoning has usually been their method of dispatch. Or they're prostitutes killing their johns."

Kunzelman nodded.

Mack looked over all of the police reports, the surveillance photos, all of the data compiled and on display at the war room in Denver FBI headquarters.

"Rarely do they engage in sexual activity," Mack continued. "Maybe mutilation, but it's usually on a male who's wronged them, or that they've perceived has wronged them."

He imagined the woman carting off these kids in the laundry cart, like dirty linen.

"Maybe she's gay," Kunzelman said.

Mack had thought about that, and dismissed it. Abduction and murder weren't crimes committed because of homosexuality. There was always a deep streak of psychopathy involved.

No, whoever this woman was in the video, she wasn't a serial killer with gender issues, or rape issues.

"She's not the killer," Mack said.

Kunzelman looked at him.

"She's the collector."

35

The very moment he decided to kill himself, Charles Starkey felt several things. The first and most powerful emotion was a profound sense of relief. It washed over him like a gentle warm wave, soothing his reeling mind and body. For the first time in days, months, years, he felt like himself.

But he also felt a calm acceptance that he had done some very bad things. Awful things. Despicable, deplorable things.

And finally, inside the core of this new and virginal being, a small resolute wish to do something about it took hold. It was the last true part of himself that still remained after the swath of destruction left by his unchecked addiction.

He sat now at his desk in the only big office at his plumbing company's building and turned to the computer. It had been a gift from the owner of The Store, just before his first major purchase. Starkey didn't know a lot about computers, but the owner of The Store had told him he needed to use it for all of his transactions, that it was loaded with all of the necessary encryptions, whatever those were, so that they could "do business" without any authorities learning about it.

Now, Starkey launched his Internet browser.

No one had ever accused him of being an intellectual giant, but Starkey knew he was smart in a more base way. Cunning, like a rodent. And like most rodents, he had a strong instinct for danger, so he knew, as his fingers hit the keyboard, that what he was about to do would not go unnoticed by the very man who had provided him the computer in the first place.

So when he typed in the web address for the FBI, Charles Starkey knew that he was doing more than just acting on his last, final wish.

He was signing his own death warrant.

36

Bernard Evans disembarked from the private jet, walked down the portable staircase, collected his bags, and made his way to a rented Cadillac. He was following the directions given to him by the people from The Store. He did not intend to deviate in any way.

Nothing would prevent him from enjoying the greatest weekend of his life.

He stowed the bags in the trunk and drove away from the airport, the route ahead clearly mapped in his mind.

Evans felt confident that he'd concealed his tracks up to this point. The forging of a flight manifest had taken some effort and required the involvement, albeit unwittingly, of others. But it had been necessary.

He was taking no chances on this one.

In fact, he nearly beamed with pride at all of his safe-guards. He was so thorough, it had always been the hall-mark of his work. What made it so much more impressive was that no one would ever discover that a crime had taken place.

The Store made guarantees to its customers and Evans

had no reason to doubt them. It had worked wonderfully so far.

Any smart business person knew, the big money came not in the occasional big purchase. But steady purchases over time by repeat customers.

That's how the rich got richer.

The car, however, was simply rented under a third party's company name, and could not be traced back to Evans, at least on paper. He had no doubt that when he was done with it, the car would be "cleaned" of all traces.

In any event, Evans followed the road ahead. He felt relaxed and excited, a slight warm buzz from the scotch on the plane. And now here he was in the early evening, darkness creeping over the world, and he felt like an explorer, going boldly into the world of the unknown. The dark, where good things happened to bad people, and bad things happened to whoever was targeted by those with money.

Evans had money.

And he had a taste for doing bad things.

He nearly laughed again and wished he had brought along a small bottle of booze for the car trip. But it was a short ride, maybe just a half hour tops. And then when he was picked up, he had no doubt his every need would be attended to. His every thirst quenched.

They had better be.

Considering how much he'd paid.

37

It had not been a good day.

Charles Starkey hurried out of the office even though it was only early afternoon. But he had accomplished very little all day, other than growing his conviction that the world was closing in on him like a shadow he had no hope of outrunning.

Now, he drove away from the office in the opposite direction of home. He couldn't help but look over his shoulder. There had been several calls on both his office phone and his cell.

Charles Starkey had answered neither.

Instead, he had spent the majority of the day pacing in his office, drinking from a bottle of vodka in his drawer and debating about calling the FBI again.

He was not good at waiting.

Starkey drove in no consistent direction, taking quick turns without using turn signals. He checked his mirrors so often he narrowly avoided hitting two parked cars.

It reminded him of the time when he was a kid and his parents had taken him to an amusement park. They had encouraged him to try out a mini roller coaster. Not the real ones. This was specifically designed for children, who filled the seats around him. He remembered the bar coming down over his body, his hands sticky from cotton candy.

And then the ride began.

The initial push had excited him as the little car picked up speed. But the first big loop found young Charles Starkey screaming at the top of his lungs. His face wet with tears, he never stopped screaming until the ride came to an end.

He had never been on another rollercoaster his entire life.

Until now.

Eventually he was confident that no one was following so at the first bar he spotted he pulled into the back lot, ensuring his car wouldn't be visible from the street. He parked and went inside.

It was a dive bar with one bartender and three customers. He went to a booth, saw the bartender roll her eyes, and he sat down. He put his cell phone on the table.

He ordered a double whiskey on the rocks and gulped from it when it arrived. It was desperation time, he knew that. It was kill himself, be killed, or rescued by the FBI.

The more he thought about it, the better he liked the idea of witness protection.

The plan would be simple.

Testify against whoever was in charge of The Store, do whatever had to be done, then go into the FBI's witness protection. Keep things under control for awhile. He could still go on the Internet, have some fun. And then, maybe after awhile, start to have some *real* fun again. Not cyber fun.

He found the bottom of his glass, and signaled the bartender for another. He knew he was drunk, but he felt mostly sick. The second drink was before him and he had a moment of dizziness. He felt like he was literally spinning until he grabbed the edges of the table with both hands and closed his eyes, squeezed them shut and ground his teeth.

When he opened them again, the spinning had stopped. He picked up the glass and drank it all down, threw a pair of twenties on the table and went out to his car. He keyed the ignition, and headed back toward his home. He had to piss, that was for sure. But maybe paranoia was getting the better of him. Could people from The Store know that he had already sent an email to the FBI? Could they be after him already? And what about the phone calls to his office? They could have been anyone.

By the time he made it back to his neighborhood, he was convinced that he could spend tonight in his own bed, and when he woke up, he would have a clearer perspective on things.

Still, just to be safe, he drove parallel to his street, and stole a glance down its length as he passed it.

That's when he saw the car.

When he had begun his dealing with the mystery men in the dark coats, borrowing money at obscenely high interest rates, he had once joked about their penchant for driving dark, Lincoln town cars. Like they were an airport shuttle service. It had seemed to him back then that every wiseguy in the city drove one.

Just like the kind that was idling about four houses down from his house.

Charles Starkey immediately understood that he was not being paranoid and he wasn't going home tonight.

STORE SECURITY

38

It had been quite easy for Butterfly to keep track of Bernard Evans' movements. She had simply placed a tracking device on the underside of the car. An unnecessary precaution, but one she made anyway. Caution, she had learned, was never overrated. It was only overrated by those without the requisite patience.

She had given Evans a specific set of driving directions that amounted to one big circuit that caused him to pass by her vantage point at least three times. It was the best way for her to make sure he hadn't been followed.

In addition to her visual confirmation, she followed the tracking device on a tablet and was satisfied that Evans was not deviating from the plan.

She had aborted previous deliveries when the buyer proved to be unreliable. There was too much at stake for everyone. No need for unnecessary risk.

Now, Butterfly waited while Evans made his last loop along the route.

At the appointed time, he pulled to a stop just up the road from her and she passed him by, flashing her headlights once. Butterfly checked her rearview mirror to make sure he was following.

In less than two minutes she led him to a nondescript building on a barren industrial lot. There were several structures on the property, all of them aluminum warehouses along with a few dumpsters and empty pallets.

Butterfly drove to the last building at the rear of the property, thumbed the door opener and pulled her vehicle inside. Once she saw that Evans had followed her in as well, she hit the control again and the door closed.

She adjusted the .45 fitted snugly in her shoulder holster, and stepped out of the shadows.

"You probably have to use the restroom," she said.

39

The Owner was home. The luxury condo was on the top floor and had been built to his specifications. He had his own communications center that operated separately from the rest of the building.

It was his lair and his fortress.

Best of all, was the view.

He had built his own living space solely around the view. And he had arranged it so that when he worked, the various computer screens and television monitors failed to block his view.

It was a glorious snapshot of Washington, but best of all, he could clearly see in the distance, one building that he never failed to single out, and relish the image before him.

The J. Edgar Hoover Building.

Headquarters of the FBI.

The monitoring system The Owner had installed was very complex. It was designed to be a cyber watchdog, continuously patrolling his own enterprise, while simultaneously keeping a close eye on anyone and everyone with whom he did business.

While the mechanics were very complex, the basic idea was simple. Every single "partner" in his enterprise was tagged. Their computers, cell phones, home phones, car phones, anything and everything they used to communicate with others was flagged. And the usage of each of those items was also monitored with a flagging system. A master list, comprehensive and thorough, was used to corroborate safe usage of the items by his customers. If one of his clients used their home computer to buy a book on Amazon, the monitoring system noticed, but did not do anything about it. If one of his clients called his distant relative's home in Flagstaff, the monitoring system noticed, but did not raise any alarms.

However, any calls to 911, or a police station, hospital, attorney's office, government entity, etc., any of those types of contacts, whether it be via cell phone, home phone, computer, and even a personal visit (the system was linked to an unofficial security camera network), the alarm was raised.

So the minute Charles Starkey, hundreds of miles away, typed the web address of the FBI into his browser window, a shower of warning lights cascaded across The Owner's main monitor.

He read the report and knew instantly what was transpiring.

The Owner sighed softly and picked up his satellite phone.

40

The two happiest days of a boat owner's life are the day he buys the boat, and the day he sells the boat.

But right now, Charles Starkey was happy to have the boat, period.

When he'd seen the mobster's car parked outside his house, he knew he could never go back. They'd already given him multiple warnings about his lack of payment. Plus, they'd clearly given up trying to reach him via phone.

They were going to hurt him, and hurt him bad. Maybe even kill him. Then try to get the life insurance money from his wife.

Well, that wasn't going to happen.

Because no one knew about the boat.

Not his wife. Not his insurance agent. Hell, no one at the marina knew it was his because he hardly ever used it. He'd gotten it because at one point in his foolish past he thought it would be a good place to take the underage prostitutes he had developed a taste for. But he'd quickly discovered that wasn't practical. Most of them wanted to have sex in a hotel

room or his car. They didn't like the idea of being transported to a boat.

So he'd given up on the fantasy, but hadn't given up
the boat.

Now, he had the power on, and was charging his cell
phone. He couldn't hide forever.

He needed to get in touch again with the FBI before his
enemies found him.

Starkey checked his phone again and there was barely
5% of battery power. He had to wait until–

The boat shifted.

He looked up from his phone.

Could it have been the water? There was no boat traffic
whatsoever in the marina.

It had seemed odd.

He wished he had a gun. There was a flare gun somewhere on board, probably near the emergency first aid kit.
But it was stowed in the bench by the captain's wheel.

He started to get up.

"Sit down," a voice said from the doorway.

Starkey looked up and found a woman watching him.
She had a gun in her hand and a face that was totally devoid
of any emotion.

"Who are you?" Starkey asked.

The woman squeezed the trigger and Starkey felt something hit him hard in the chest and he struggled to breathe.
He saw the gun spurt flame again but didn't hear anything.

He wanted to ask the woman if she was from the Mob.

But his last thought was an answer.

She wasn't.

She was from The Store.

41

Rebecca Spencer sat on the edge of her bed, trying to think. She instinctively knew the cabin, or cell as she thought of it, had been thoroughly stripped so as not to provide any type of weapon.

No phone. No unlocked doors. Just the bed, a toilet, and a sink.

It was not her style to wait.

Although it seemed like they had no intention of harming her, that they were basically storing her until the ransom money came in, she wasn't about to sit around and wait.

She needed a weapon.

Rebecca considered the bed.

She stepped back, lifted the mattress and looked at the metal frame, thinking maybe there were springs she could bend into some type of shiv, like they do in prison movies.

But beneath the mattress all she saw were two strips of metal welded to the frame.

"Damn it," she said.

She put the mattress back down, sat on it, and studied the floor.

It was wood. She believed it was called tongue and groove – solid.

The walls were wood planks as well. And there was nothing in the bathroom. She'd already looked at that.

No windows.

Rebecca looked at the headboard. It really wasn't a headboard – just a metal bar that connected the sides of the frame.

She was turning her head away when she caught a glimpse of something dark on the wall.

Rebecca pulled the bed away and looked at it.

It was a knot in the wood of one of the planks that made the wall. And at the top of the knot was a small hole.

But the knot was at the bottom of the plank.

It reminded Rebecca of something.

When she was in grade school, a boy named Pat Bobryk had a crush on her. One day after school, they were sitting with some friends on the outfield grass of the baseball field. The fence that marked the outfield was made of wire and wood. The wire ran horizontally, and thick planks of wood made vertical slats in the fence. At the top, the wood slats stuck about six inches above the highest part of the wire.

So Pat decided to hurdle the fence as a way of showing off in front of Rebecca. He ran, jumped, and his front foot hit one of the slats dead on, and it broke in half vertically, leaving a jagged point that proceeded to scrape along Pat's hamstring and open up a gash at least a foot long.

The boy needed 42 stitches to close it back up.

Now, Rebecca looked at the knot at the base of that plank behind the bed.

She wondered. *If I kicked it just right, and hard enough, would it split? And if so, where?*

Rebecca pulled the bed farther out, and pushed it to the side, then sat on the floor and shimmied up to the wall so that her feet were pressed against the wall.

She leaned to the side and looked again at the knot and the small hole at its top.

Rebecca rested her heel just above the knot and traced a line of grain in the wood that ran up and to the left with its origin in the hole.

It was a guess, but if she kicked it just right, and hard enough, the plank might split along the line of grain. And if it broke loose, the result would be a long sharp piece of wood.

A weapon.

Rebecca brought her knee back, tilted the top of her foot toward her so that her heel was leading, exhaled, then drove her heel straight backward.

The sound was insanely loud in the empty, quiet space, and she felt a stab of pain in her foot.

She looked at the wall.

The wood had cracked, but it was still in place.

Rebecca gritted her teeth and kicked again.

This time, the plank cracked inwardly, in two uneven shapes that reminded her of Vermont and New Hampshire.

She got on her knees and went to the wall.

There was enough room for her to put a finger into the hole above the knot. She slid it in, then hooked the wood and pulled it toward her. It was dry, but still strong.

It wouldn't move.

She studied the plank again. The crack was as she hoped – ending in a jagged point, but she had to break it loose without breaking the plank horizontally.

Rebecca leaned back, brought her foot forward and kicked one more time.

The plank popped and the two pieces were fully apart.

She reached in, and carefully broke the piece free.

It was wide at the base, and ended in a narrow, jagged point.

She touched the tip with her finger.

It was sharp enough to break skin.

She thought of the back of Pat Bobryk's thigh, the way it had been sliced clean open.

Oh yeah, she thought.

Bring it on, bitches.

42

Mack left Denver by the direct order of Hopestil Fletcher and landed in D.C. after an uneventful flight. He powered on his cell phone and checked for messages. There was one from Adelia letting him know everything was going fine at home without him. She had said it and then chuckled.

He smiled, put the phone away, collected his bag and slid into the backseat of a Bureau car.

A half hour later they pulled up in front of the Hoover Building.

Inside, he went directly to the Computer Crimes section where a young assistant with the odd name of Merlin showed him to a war room.

Inside, there were half a dozen computers linked by various cables.

A woman stood before a large screen. A keyboard sat on a raised pedestal and the woman was furiously typing away. Mack noted that she wore black, polished cowboy boots, blue jeans, an Oakland Raiders T-shirt underneath a black sportcoat.

She glanced at him.

"Who are you?"

"Wallace Mack."

The woman nodded, then looked at the two other people in the room. "Give us a minute, would you?" she said to them.

They snatched up their coffee cups and left the room quickly, shutting the door behind them.

Mack sat down at the table, caught a whiff of vanilla flavored coffee from whoever had been sitting there.

"Who are you?" Mack asked her.

"I'm Moody," she said. "Don't bother with a joke, I've heard them all."

Mack smiled at her.

"A tip came in that eventually found its way to me," she said. "I understand you're here to help connect the dots."

"That's right, hopefully," Mack said.

"The tip was initially dismissed," Moody continued. "It was somewhat mysterious and unbelievable, until we traced it via the IP address to a certain individual with a proclivity for sexual escapades with minors."

"And who would that be?" Mack asked.

"His name is Charles Starkey and he's a real prize," she said. "Rich from his father's plumbing business, he had a host of charges for assault, improper contact and various degrees of sexual assault with children."

"Why is he still running around?"

"Because he has good lawyers, and apparently has kept his nose clean for a few years now."

"So who did the tip come from?"

"This is where it gets interesting. Charles Starkey provided the information."

Mack frowned. "Why?"

"Well, we dug into his financial records and what we found was complete chaos," Moody said. She tapped on the keyboard and a screen came to life behind her. Mack could see various financial statements that meant nothing to him.

"Funds being moved around with dizzying speed but eventually we were able to tease out that he's blown through all of his money and is deep in debt. To the wrong people."

"Loan sharks? The Mob?"

Moody nodded.

"So he said he wanted to make a deal," she said. "He supposedly knows about an Internet ring that sells kids online. And that he'll tell us everything he knows in exchange for going into the Witness Protection Program."

"Is this Internet ring connected to the Mob?"

"We don't know. Yet."

"This is all great and everything," Mack said. "But how does this apply to me?"

"Well, in his message, he says that he recognized one of the girls on sale in The Store."

"The Store?"

"That's what they call it, I guess."

Mack suddenly knew.

"Rebecca Spencer."

Moody pointed at him and said, "That's correct. Starkey claims she was listed on The Store and that he figures a lot of people are looking for her. He's hoping that his information will help us find her and we'll reward him with immunity."

"Let's give it to him."

"We plan to. If we can find him."

"What?"

"He's missing."

"Great."

"And that's not all."

Mack waited.

"He said that the Spencer girl wasn't on the site long. Someone bought her right away."

EMPLOYEE OF THE WEEK

43

Butterfly landed in Cheyenne, Wyoming, after a flight from New York to Chicago that included new tickets in different names.

The Owner had arranged it all.

Now, she left the Wyoming airport in a rental car, also rented under an alias, and headed toward Colorado.

The kill cabin was actually closer to Denver than Cheyenne, but she didn't like to fly into the same airport too many times. Besides, the drive from Cheyenne wasn't bad at all.

The business in New Jersey had gone well, and she'd ditched the gun in the ocean, about a mile up from where she'd killed Starkey and blown up his boat.

Butterfly recognized the man as a recent visitor to the compound. He must have crossed the Owner.

It took her a little under five hours to get to the enclosure, having passed miles upon miles of vast stretches of prairie punctuated by rolling hills and bluffs, and enormous herds of cattle warming up in the sun.

Now, she turned into the paved driveway of the executive cabin. It was where she had stashed Bernard Evans, while she dashed off to Jersey. It wasn't an anomaly. Sometimes the customers liked to stay a day or two in the executive cabin while their "purchase" was carefully prepared.

Evans had been pretty drunk when she dropped him there.

There was a small staff at the executive cabin, who were given strict orders not to access the other sections of the compound. The employees included a cook and a cleaning woman.

Butterfly provided security.

Like the staff, guests were not permitted to leave the grounds of the executive cabin.

Now, Butterfly parked the rental car, retrieved her small travel bag and went inside.

She used her key card to open a door that led to her area. The only place she really called home.

She stashed her travel bag, splashed some water on her face and went to her gun safe.

Butterfly entered the combination, the door opened, and she stepped inside. Her eyes caressed the selection of weapons. There were handguns, rifles, revolvers, hideout guns, even a whole wall of "throwaway" guns – with their serial numbers removed so she could dump them without fear of a trace.

She put on a shoulder holster with a S&W .40 automatic, then left her section of the lodge and headed for the bar. Sure enough, she found Bernard Evans there with a glass of amber liquid in front of him.

Butterfly took the seat next to him.

The bartender, who also doubled as part of the kitchen

staff, nodded at her and placed a glass of sparkling water in front of her.

"When will I get to see her?" Evans asked.

Butterfly looked into the bottom of her glass.

"How about now?" she said.

44

M ack knew that pornographers were always on the cutting edge of computer technology. They were the ones who had pioneered VHS, then DVDs and then online movies.

And the more deviant they were, the more adept they became at hiding their online activities.

Mack recalled less than a year ago, a child porn ring, all online, had been busted. There had been some twenty-seven thousand subscribers, worldwide to the network.

The only way to catch them was to get a crack in the armor.

And Charles Starkey had provided that glimpse.

"Are you getting his computer?" Mack asked.

Moody nodded.

"We've got a team on the way."

Just then, the door opened, and one of the assistants who'd been ushered out, came back into the conference room.

"Bad news," he said.

Mack and Moody waited.

"Our team was on the way to Starkey's house when they pulled over to let fire trucks go by."

"Oh, Christ."

The man nodded. "The house went up in flames, with all of Starkey's family inside."

"Jesus," Mack said.

"There's more."

"Of course there is," Moody said.

"A boat in the local marina blew up with a body inside. They think it's Starkey."

45

"That's all right," Moody said, casually dismissing the demise of Charles Starkey. "We don't need his physical computer or network to track him."

Mack realized that Moody was all business. No time for compassion. Maybe that's what drew her to computers. And the Oakland Raiders.

"Get everyone in here, now," she barked at the assistant.

Moments later, the room was full of techies listening as Moody barked out orders.

Hopestil Fletcher came to the door and beckoned Mack out.

"The Spencers are not happy," she said.

"Do you want me to talk to them?" he asked.

"No, I want you to put together a profile of who is behind The Store. It's got to be one person."

"I know how to catch him," Mack said.

"How?"

"Tracking computer files is next to impossible, no matter how good Moody is," Mack said.

"She's the best in the world, Mac."

"I know. But there's one thing that's much easier to follow."

"The money," Fletcher said.

Mack nodded.

"The odds are the perp is male," Mack said. "He's got a history of sex crimes, that probably stopped some time ago. A knack for computers or a history of hacking. And in the last few days, a huge influx of money."

"I've got a team looking already, but I'll make sure they're looped into what Moody is doing. How much do you think he's taken in?"

"Start with five million in the last few days."

46

"We've got something," Moody said.

Fletcher and Mack sat among the techies, looking at the big screen on the wall, with a blizzard of numbers and computer code.

Suddenly, one of the strings was highlighted by Moody.

"This is Starkey's money going out," she explained. "It hit first at a bank account in the Caymans. From there it was broken up and sent out into nearly a hundred different amounts, each amount being transferred dozens of times."

Mack knew they might never find the money, but they could sure as hell follow it.

Moody continued. "However, we figured that the amounts must have regrouped at some point, so we picked two to follow. They ended up back in the Caymans, to an account registered to M. Stohr Enterprises."

Mack shook his head.

"The Murder Store," he said.

Moody looked at him oddly, then nodded.

"Here's the best part," she continued. "Guess where we tracked it to?"

The hum of the computer equipment was the only sound in the room.

"Right here. Washington, D.C."

47

B ernard Evans felt more alive than he'd felt when he first became a multi- millionaire.

Even partially hungover, the taste of last night's scotch still in his mouth, he felt positively electric with a thirst for what would soon happen making him practically jump out of bed.

Evans thought about the money he'd spent, and that it was going to be more than worth it. In fact, he thought about his company's IPO and how the stock was doing.

He could sell off another batch in a few months and buy another girl.

Which reminded him...

The rules about coming to this place had been very clear. No cell phones. No laptops. Nothing with a wireless connection. Which made sense because there was no Internet service here anyway.

But Evans was a tech geek.

And he had figured that for his own safety, he should have something with him just in case he needed to call someone, like his assistant, in an emergency.

Plus, he needed his protégé Reese Stocker, to be able to reach him in an all-out catastrophe.

So he had broken apart his phone, taken the battery out, and taken apart his travel clock that he favored on business trips.

He'd then placed the components of his phone into the rear compartment of the clock.

The woman, the crazy chick, hadn't bothered to check. Even though she'd run the bags through an X-ray deal like the security people at airports had.

Now, he reassembled the phone, clicked the battery into place and powered it up. After a few moments, he was pleased to see that the battery was nearly seventy-five percent charged.

He fired up his brokerage account's app, and checked the balance of his portfolio.

$123 million.

Oh yes, he thought.

He had plenty to make another purchase.

And soon.

So he slid the phone into his pocket and when the scary chick came around, the one who called herself Butterfly, he was ready. But sometimes being with this woman felt like a cold wet blanket thrown on him because he felt like he could tell she despised him for what he was.

At least, that's what he had initially thought. But now, standing with her, having just looked into her eyes, he realized that what made her so scary was her utter lack of feeling. She didn't despise him. Because she didn't really see him as a person. Evans got the feeling that she could reach up and slit his throat and her expression wouldn't change.

Evans followed her to a walled compound with a security gate.

The woman swiped a card and the door's lock snicked open.

The area was a wide expanse of lawn with several small cottages spread haphazardly around the area. They were small, like the kind of rustic motel cabins in the country.

The woman walked directly to the cabin the farthest from the door.

Evans felt his heart beating faster as they approached.

The woman got to the cottage and Evans saw that the cabin's door had the same kind of security system. Butterfly swiped her card again and Evans followed her in.

The girl was sitting on the bed, her hands in her lap.

Evans stopped breathing.

She was everything he'd hoped for.

And more.

48

The FBI's rapid response team led the way, followed by Mack and a few other agents, as well as some D.C. cops.

The address was a brownstone near Georgetown.

According to records, the house was owned by a shell corporation called H. Cide Enterprises.

The guy was good at mass murder, not so much at stand-up comedy, Mack thought.

He hung back and watched the armed response team in action. They hit the front door, announced themselves, then used a battering ram to knock the door inward.

The team raced inside and Mack heard what deep down he suspected they might find.

Silence.

When the all-clear was given, Mack entered the building.

It was a beautiful brownstone with lovely hardwood floors, immaculately painted trim and wainscoting.

The ceilings were high, the windows large and beautiful, letting in a tremendous amount of light.

It was also completely empty.

No furniture. No people.

Nothing.

Except for two items in the middle of the living room.

The first was a dead man hanging by the neck from an exposed beam. He was dressed like an office worker on casual Friday. Khakis and a dress shirt. He was in his socks with a pair of penny loafers beneath him.

Judging by his face and the odor in the room, he had been dead for at least several days.

The other item sat on the floor next to the dead man, a dozen feet or so from the breathtaking marble fireplace.

A complex system of hard drives. They were all connected and Mack watched the blinking green and yellow lights on a sophisticated display.

Mack's phone buzzed and he answered as crime scene techs began arriving and taking control of the room.

It was Hopestil Fletcher.

"His name is Terry Piechura," she said. "Moody tracked him down. He was a hacker turned investor. Very wealthy but with an almost invisible past. All we know right now is that he and a woman named Chloe Jamison were charged as juveniles with a series of escalating crimes and then they both disappeared.

"She's the Collector," Mack said without hesitation. "The janitor who snatched Rebecca Spencer was a woman. It's got to be her. And judging by the setup here–"

He paused.

"Mack?" Fletcher asked.

"How did Moody track him down so fast?" he asked.

"What the hell does that mean?" Fletcher said. "She's the best we've got in cyber crimes. She's a genius."

Mack shook his head.

"Have her double-check the trail that led her to this guy. Did any of it recently come online?"

He heard Fletcher sigh.

"What is it, Mack?"

Mack walked away from the room and back out onto the street. "Listen, I've tracked these guys all my life. They don't commit suicide. They just don't. Sure, there has been a case or two, but ninety-nine percent of the time, they don't."

He thought back to some of his cases.

" They see themselves as victims, forced to kill by other people," he continued. "There is no guilt. No fear of prison."

"So you're saying this is a set-up?" Fletcher said.

As he spoke the words, he suddenly realized how strong his conviction was.

"Yes, it absolutely is."

FINAL LIQUIDATION

49

Bernard Evans' hands were shaking he was so excited.

The girl was beautiful. Better and sexier than anything he could have imagined.

"Hello," he said.

She looked at him, her face set in stone.

He approached her, saw the table in the next room with his favorite bottle of scotch, and some assorted toys, including a riding crop, handcuffs, ball gags, cock rings, butt plugs and nipple clamps.

Evans felt himself getting hard.

He approached the beautiful girl and placed his hand along her cheek.

She looked up at him, her face meek. Her eyes terrified.

She was warm.

And then he slapped her.

It was a quick backhand that rocked the girl's head and snapped her neck backward.

Evans went to the table and poured himself some scotch.

He was going to take his time with this one.

Get every penny's worth.

50

M ack was back in Moody's workspace. There was a big picture of Einstein with the tagline "Think Different" and the Apple logo.

"I've got a team rechecking the information that led us to Piechura," she said. "In the meantime, I'm focusing on finding that girl."

"Good. I have a feeling both avenues will lead us to her," Mack said.

"The best way in was through Starkey's system. From there, it was easy to crack the first layers. But after that, things got quite a bit more complicated."

Mack pulled a chair up next to Moody's elaborate workstation.

"We're crawling the trail," she said.

"How?" Mack asked.

"It's too complicated for me to thoroughly explain. Let me put it this way, whoever built this system knew what they were doing. They created millions of dead ends and false paths so that no one could find out where the money ends up. Now, some bright young man years back invented these things called spiders, in cyber form, that do nothing other than scurry along all of these paths, looking for daylight, so to speak. Most spiders would never be able to find their way through this. But since we're part of the government and we actually employ the best hackers in the world, we don't have ordinary spiders. We have super spiders."

"Super spiders," Mack echoed.

"Yes. There are several species of super spider employed by the FBI. Each breed does something a little bit differently than the others. I mentioned that most of them were designed to chase down blind leads."

"Yes," Mack said.

"Well, there is another kind that instead of hunting, is a little bit more of a gatherer."

"What does it gather?"

"To keep it simple, I'll call them data points," Moody explained. "Basically, as the other spiders rule out some of the dead ends, these gatherers then go about throwing a cyber ring around the remaining possibilities and look for shared data, in pattern form. The more points that coincide, the clearer the pattern. In this case, one pattern seems to have become clear."

"What's the pattern?"

"Cell phones."

Mack was surprised. He hadn't expected something as mundane as cell phones to be a key discovery in an intense cyber hunt.

Moody nodded. "I won't explain the algorithm because it would take hours, but basically at the same time some of these switchbacks were activated, a corresponding activity almost always followed suit, via cell phones."

"So who do the phones belong to?"

"It's not that easy," Moody said. "They are no longer in service. Probably disposable. But while we can't say who they were, we can say where."

She turned to a map and pointed to Colorado.

"Right here."

It took only a moment to realize that she was pointing to nearly the exact same spot on the map where the bodies had been found.

51

Evans was ready.

He wanted to be patient, but he also knew that he had limited time.

He walked over to the girl who was still sitting on the bed. He grabbed her hair, pulled her face toward him and kissed her as she struggled to pull away from him.

"I'm going to fuck you so many times your pussy will be worn out," he whispered to her. He licked his lips. She tasted like sugar.

He grabbed her by the throat, pushed her back onto the bed, rolled her over and pulled down her pants.

Evans gasped. Her ass was creamy white, milky like a farm girl.

The girl was flat on her stomach, her arms spread wide over the bed.

Evans unbuckled his pants.

He dropped his pants to the floor, then his underwear. He stroked his dick.

He climbed onto the bed and straddled the girl.

This was going to be-

Evans felt the girl twist underneath him and he was glad. He liked it better when they fought.

But then he realized the girl was on her side and her arm was coming up from the edge of the bed.

There was something in it.

He felt a stabbing pain in his side and looked down to see a piece of wood buried in his side.

Evans suddenly had trouble breathing.

It was like some giant weight was on his chest.

The girl pushed him off the bed and he landed on the floor, looked up as he saw the girl swing a lamp at his head. It connected.

Then darkness.

52

M ack picked up the phone and got Fletcher on the line.

"What is it?" she said.

"Moody found the trail back to Colorado, near the site where the kids' bodies were discovered."

"So what are you thinking?" she said.

"I'm thinking that's where the killing location is," he said. "I think people put in orders online, and then arrangements are made for the killing to take place somewhere in Colorado. And that's where they dispose of the bodies."

"What do you need?"

"We've got a team scrambling from Denver. Who knows what they're going to find out there."

"Are you still not buying that suicide?" she asked him.

"Absolutely not. The more I think about it, the more convinced I am that whoever is behind this is way too smart for something like that. I think they knew we were getting close and they made a sacrifice to throw us off the trail."

"Or maybe it was one of those rare instances where the psychopath finally does kill himself."

Mack realized she was just playing devil's advocate.

"No. This isn't over," he said.

53

Rebecca was shaking. She couldn't believe what she was seeing. A guy on the floor surrounded by blood, and now bleeding from the head. His eyes were wide open, too.

Had she killed him?

She didn't know. But what she did know was that if that woman came back and found the guy dead, well, Rebecca had a pretty good idea of what would happen.

The woman would kill her, no doubt.

This was no political kidnapping with a ransom involved. Rebecca understood that, now.

All along, they had planned to do horrible things to her.

Which meant she had to find a way to get out.

Rebecca tried the door but it was locked, as were all of the windows.

She went back to the dead man on the floor.

His pants were still on the floor, too. She picked them up and dug through the pockets, nothing. Completely empty.

How could that be?

Then she remembered that he had gone into the other room.

Rebecca went to the table where she saw what she instantly understood to be sex toys.

And there, at the edge of the table, was a wallet, some car keys and a phone.

But the phone wasn't a cell phone, she could tell that. It was a little bigger and heavier.

Her heart was beating a million miles a minute as she picked it up, realized it was off, and powered it on.

It felt like an eternity waiting for the phone to power up. Were there cameras in the cabin? Probably.

She looked around but didn't see any.

At last the phone lit up and she looked at the display.

It was a touch screen.

But not like one she'd seen before.

Still, she managed to call up the keypad.

She hit 9-1-1 and pressed the phone to her ear.

Surprisingly, she heard a voice on the other end of the line.

GOING OUT OF BUSINESS

"We just got a 9-1-1 call from a girl claiming to be Rebecca Spencer," an agent announced in the middle of the war room.

"Is it her?" Mack asked. "Verification?"

"We don't know," the agent said.

Mack looked at Moody. "Does the location match?"

The room fell silent.

"Yes," Moody said.

Immediately the room descended into a frenzy of activity as the exact location was sent to the SWAT team which had already been scrambled from Denver.

"It's a remote location," the agent said. "We're choppering them in. They should be there in about twenty minutes. We'll have full audio and video here," he said pointing to the screen in the war room.

"Tell them to hurry," Mack said. "And be careful. There may be someone waiting for them."

There was a camera in the cabin.

With a feed that led to a control room in Butterfly's compound.

The problem was, after Evans had slapped the girl and gone to get a drink, Butterfly had stopped watching.

It wasn't that she couldn't watch, far from it. But the murderous rampages had become boring and commonplace to her.

So once she knew that Evans was locked in the cabin with the girl, she didn't really care what happened. Still, it was part of her job to monitor, and make sure nothing went wrong.

All Butterfly had done was check her encrypted computer for messages from The Owner, then stripped and cleaned her Colt 911.

After that, she went and took a look at the monitor.

It took her a moment to realize what she was seeing. The customer, Bernard Evans, on his back on the cabin floor, surrounded by blood, some sort of long, jagged piece of wood sticking out of his side and a lamp on the floor next to his head.

The girl, standing in the middle of the room with a SAT phone in her hand.

Butterfly felt a brief moment of disbelief, and realized she had made a second mistake. How had Evans gotten a SAT phone past her?

She shook her head, fear beginning to tingle throughout her, and then a vibration ran through her body, followed by a thrumming sound in her ear.

And then she made yet another realization.

Choppers.

56

It wasn't her capture. Or the interminable time spent in the back of a vehicle. It wasn't even killing the man. He deserved that. No, years later, when Rebecca looked back at her ordeal, one thing stood out as the most terrifying moment.

The waiting.

She stood in the middle of the cabin, the SAT phone in her hand, the dead man on the floor behind her.

There was no way out. The door was locked and she guessed it could only be opened from the outside with one of the cards the woman had used.

Rebecca stood in the room. The phone in one hand. The shard of wood in the other. She had pulled it out of the dead man's body.

The sound of helicopters reached her ears and a faint glimmer of hope blossomed inside her chest.

She watched as blood dripped from the piece of wood onto the cabin's floor.

And then she heard the sound of footsteps outside.

An image of the woman flashed in front of Rebecca's eyes.

She gripped the piece of wood so hard it cut into her hand.

If it was the woman, Rebecca would throw herself at her, no matter what. Even if the woman had a gun.

Rebecca didn't care.

She would rather die than be a captive again.

57

There was no hesitation on Butterfly's part.

She had grabbed her bag even as a message came through on her phone. It was the worst news she could have gotten.

Butterfly ran.

Out of her cabin, through the back woods and down a steep draw.

There was a vehicle five miles away accessible only through the steepest terrain and far enough from the cabin to avoid detection yet close enough to a rural highway.

With effortless ease, she slid the backpack onto her shoulders mid-stride and ran beneath the thick canopy of trees toward the waiting vehicle. It was a trail she was familiar with as it was part of her daily training routine. She knew every bump in the trail and now, she ran it faster than ever before.

For years she had been devoid of most emotion. But now, as she ran, a tear escaped the corner of her eye. A murderous rage rose inside her.

Her friend, the only human being in the world she had allowed herself to love, was gone.

The message that had come through on her phone told her that. It was a code they had agreed on should either one be in danger of being killed or captured.

But he had included one more piece of information.

The name of the person responsible for their downfall.

58

"They had to break a door down, but they got her," the agent said.

Mack was watching through the helmet cam of one of the SWAT team members. All he could see was a clearing with a collection of small cabins and what looked like a main house.

"Must have been some kind of resort. Or hunting lodge," Mack said. "Let's find out who owns it, immediately."

"We've got an ID on the dead man," another agent said, a phone pressed to his ear. "Bernard Evans, CEO of Burn Software."

"Jesus," Mack said.

"This is interesting," Moody said.

Mack walked over to where the computer specialist stood, in front of a large computer screen showing rapidly radiating codes and symbols.

"What is it?" Mack said.

"One of the spiders had gone directly to Evans' network."

"That makes sense if he was one of the customers," Mack said.

"I know but here's what's interesting. Someone is killing the spiders and shutting down the system."

Mack considered that for a moment.

"Could Evans have preprogrammed his network to self-destruct if he was caught?" he asked.

"No, a lot of it can be automated, but what you're seeing here is someone manipulating these searches in real-time."

"Can you tell if they're shutting down Evans' network, or the entire Store network?"

"Everything is being shut down."

He thought about it. If the person closing down the system was an ally of Evans, the focus would be Evans' history.

And then it hit Mack all at once.

He knew what was going on.

"Shit," he said.

"Someone didn't set us up. They set him up," he said, pointing to the screen of the now dead Bernard Evans.

59

Reese Stocker sat on the sand on the coast of Belize, watching the waves roll in. He had a glass of rum in his hand and the thought brought a smile to his face. He hadn't had a drink of rum in years. Doing it now, he felt like a pirate.

He was glad to be out of Silicon Valley, happy to have exacted his revenge on Bernard Evans.

Most of all, he was glad he had gotten away with it.

With his computer skill, discovering what Evans had been up to was easy. Finding the owner of the Store had taken a lot more time and effort. And then selling some of his stock in Burn in order to fund the killing of Terry Piechura had been even more difficult.

But Bernard Evans had been a genius. And he had told Stocker many, many times that money could buy anything.

Anything.

In this case, it had bought Reese Stocker the sweetest revenge known to man. Because Burn had been *his* idea. Not Evans's.

Evans had ripped him off, stolen the spotlight, used his technical genius to take over the company.

So Stocker did what he did best. Avoided a face-to-face confrontation and used his massive intelligence to program a solution.

Setting up the crazy hacker who'd come up with Store was the most dangerous part. Stocker knew the man had a partner, people who probably did the guy's dirty work.

But like all great ideas, there was risk involved.

In this case, the potential rewards won out.

Now, he was on the beach with hundreds of millions of dollars in hidden bank accounts and a foolproof identity.

Maybe he would get a part-time job. Like an anonymous offer to help law enforcement better police the Internet.

"Ha!" he laughed out loud.

There was no one around.

He owned near a half-mile of beach here. It was as private as beachfront property could get.

A shadow crossed the sun and he momentarily missed the warmth. But the sun was there, over the horizon.

He looked up, into the face of a startling beautiful woman.

She smiled at him.

But the gleam that flashed in his eye wasn't from her smile. It was from a long knife held in her right hand.

"They call me Butterfly," she said.

"You don't–" Stocker began to say.

Butterfly drove the knife directly into Stocker's heart.

"Yes," she said. "Yes I do."

Read the next Wallace Mack Thriller now:

FINDERS KILLERS

ALSO BY DAN AMES

A HARD MAN TO FORGET (THE JACK REACHER CASES: AUTHORIZED BY LEE CHILD)

DEAD WOOD (John Rockne Mystery #1)

HARD ROCK (John Rockne Mystery #2)

COLD JADE (John Rockne Mystery #3)

LONG SHOT (John Rockne Mystery #4)

EASY PREY (John Rockne Mystery #5)

BODY BLOW (John Rockne Mystery #6)

THE KILLING LEAGUE (Wallace Mack Thriller #1)

THE MURDER STORE (Wallace Mack Thriller #2)

FINDERS KILLERS (Wallace Mack Thriller #3)

DEATH BY SARCASM (Mary Cooper Mystery #1)

MURDER WITH SARCASTIC INTENT (Mary Cooper Mystery #2)

GROSS SARCASTIC HOMICIDE (Mary Cooper Mystery #3)

KILLER GROOVE (Rockne & Cooper Mystery #1)

BEER MONEY (Burr Ashland Mystery #1)

THE CIRCUIT RIDER (Circuit Rider #1)

KILLER'S DRAW (Circuit Rider #2)

TO FIND A MOUNTAIN (A WWII Thriller)

STANDALONE THRILLERS:

THE RECRUITER

KILLING THE RAT

HEAD SHOT

THE BUTCHER

BOX SETS:

AMES TO KILL

GROSSE POINTE PULP

GROSSE POINTE PULP 2

TOTAL SARCASM

WALLACE MACK THRILLER COLLECTION

SHORT STORIES:

THE GARBAGE COLLECTOR

BULLET RIVER

SCHOOL GIRL

HANGING CURVE

SCALE OF JUSTICE

AFTERWORD

For special offers, free ebooks, exclusive content and to hear about new releases, sign up for

The Official Dan Ames Reader Group at:

AuthorDanAmes.com

ABOUT THE AUTHOR

Dan Ames is a USA TODAY bestselling author and winner of the Independent Book Award for Crime Fiction.

www.authordanames.com
dan@authordanames.com

Made in the USA
Las Vegas, NV
02 May 2021

22358759R00116